DECEPTION

I0674086

Lillian Duncan

DECEPTION

Cover Art by *Kim Mendoza*

Harbourlight Books, a division of Pelican Ventures, LLC
www.pelicanbookgroup.com PO Box 1738 *Aztec, NM * 87410

Harbourlight Books sail and mast logo is a trademark of Pelican Ventures, LLC

Publishing History
First Harbourlight Edition, 2011
Print Edition ISBN 978-1-61116-147-2
Electronic Edition ISBN 978-1-61116-146-5
Published in the United States of America

Dedication

To Ronny, I couldn't do it without you! Your support and encouragement keep me writing.

To Jay, you made a difference.

Praise for *Pursued*

This is one of the best Christian fiction books I've read - definitely the best suspense/drama book I've read in the Christian genre. Lillian Duncan is a good writer, and her strong character is evident throughout the book. ~ *Chad Young,* author of *Authenticity: Real Faith in a Phony, Superficial World*

Duncan's story was deliciously romantic and breathtakingly paced. Her characters were wonderfully portrayed and I was drawn into Reggie's plight from the moment an ex-English teacher businessman drops her firm over a misplaced word. Those readers who enjoy some great kissing in between bullets and prayers will enjoy *Pursued.* ~ *Lisa Lickel,* co-author of *A Summer in Oakville*

1

Patti Jakowski sat alone at her deck watching the drizzle from the leaky roof form an ever growing puddle on her picnic table. Taking another sip of the now cold coffee, she frowned. It would be the third time she'd contacted the roofers. She would never let herself be talked into a major house renovation from a door-to-door salesman again.

Great way to start summer vacation. Sitting and watching the rain.

The ringing of the phone brought her to her feet, and she ran into the kitchen. The scent of baking cinnamon rolls reminded her to check the oven after the call. "Hello."

"Me want my aunt." It was a young girl. By the sound of her voice, maybe three, or four.

"Oh, I'm sorry, honey. You must have dialed the wrong number. Hang up and try again. OK, sweetie?" instructed Patti, slipping into her teacher voice.

"I need my aunt. Mommy's not here," said the little girl. "I 'sposed to call my aunt. I want my mommy."

Her heart skipped a beat. Patti didn't like the sound of that. Surely, her parents hadn't left this little girl alone. "You're mommy's not home with you?" Concern edged into her voice.

"Just me. Can't find Mommy. Where's Mommy?"

The little girl's voice trembled.

"I don't know, sweetie. How old are you?" Patti asked, while reaching for the pad and pen by the phone.

"I'm four." The little girl's voice was tinged with pride at the announcement.

"That's very good. What's your name?"

"I not 'spose to tell strangers." It came out more like a wail than words.

"That's a good girl. You're right, you shouldn't tell strangers your name, but I'm not a stranger. You called me, remember?"

There was a pause as the little girl considered this new information. "Sabina."

"Do you mean Sabrina?"

"Yeah, Sabina."

Patti smiled. She'd had a cat named Sabrina when she was young. Patti and her twin had played house with that silly animal for hours on end.

Her sister always said she would name her first daughter after...

Patti's heart skipped a beat. It couldn't be. Patti shook the thought away. This Sabrina had nothing to do with Patti's twin. It was a coincidence, nothing more. There were lots of little girls with the name. A little voice told her there was no such thing as coincidences. Patti ignored the little voice. "That's a pretty name, Sabrina. What's your mommy's name?"

"Mommy."

Patti resisted the urge to sigh, glad she worked with high school students instead of younger children. "Does she have another name, Sabrina?"

"No, just Mommy."

Patti looked up at the ceiling. This wasn't going

anywhere. The authorities needed to get to this little girl's house. Why hadn't she taken the time to get the caller ID on her phone set up?

"Can you tell me your aunt's name?"

"I forget." The girl's whimpers turned into sobs.

"That's OK, Sabrina. Don't cry. You're being very brave. What I want you to do is to hang up and wait by the phone until it rings. Then, make sure you pick it up, OK? It will be me calling you back."

"Otay," the little voice said.

Patti waited to hear the disconnection but nothing happened.

"Sabrina, hang up the phone. I promise to call you back."

"Otay."

This time Patti heard the disconnection. She hung up the phone, and then immediately picked it up and dialed *67.

A mechanical voice came on. "I'm sorry the number has been blocked."

"Oh, perfect," Patti mumbled. Her idea hadn't been all that great. She flopped on a kitchen chair. What was she supposed to do? She had to help this little girl.

She jumped back up as a whiff of cinnamon scented the air. Opening the oven, she pulled out the cookie sheet, found a spatula and transferred the rolls onto a plate. Another idea popped into her head. She picked up the phone and hit 0.

"Operator. How can I help you?"

Patti explained the situation and was put on hold. She ran fingers through her hair in an attempt to comb it. A haircut was one of the first things on her to-do list now that school was over for the summer.

The operator came back on after several minutes. "We'd like your permission to access your phone records to find out where the little girl called from. Just a reminder, this call is being recorded."

"Of course."

"Thank you, ma'am." The operator hung up.

Patti squeezed vanilla icing out of the plastic container and munched on slightly burnt cinnamon rolls.

Just because her name was Sabrina didn't mean she had anything to do with Jamie.

Patti hadn't heard from her twin in years. Her foot tapped against the chair rail.

The phone rang again.

"Hello."

"Who dis?"

Relief flooded Patti's soul as she heard Sabrina's little voice. "This is Patti."

"Aunt Patti. I called you. You didn't call me back. You promised," Sabrina whined.

"I know I did, Sabrina, but my phone wouldn't work. I'm not your aunt, but I'm going to find her for you."

"But you Aunt Patti. Mommy told me to call you."

Patti felt a chill at the little girl's certainty. It couldn't be…could it?

"Where do you live, sweetie?"

"Me live at home. Where you live?"

"I live in Cleveland, Sabrina. What's the name of your city?" Patti didn't know how to help without knowing where the girl was calling from.

"I gotta go potty. Bye."

"Wait, don't hang…" Patti groaned when she heard the click.

2

After her third cup of coffee, Patti sat at her kitchen table tapping her fingers on the green tile that didn't match the rest of her blue kitchen.

The operator had discovered the source of the call and assured Patti the police were on their way to the little girl's house.

Patti hoped Sabrina's mom would be there when the police arrived, and the problem would be solved.

"Of all the days to rain," she muttered as she stared out the window. Her tradition of using the first day of summer vacation to plant flowers wouldn't be happening that day—unless she wanted to crawl around in knee-deep mud.

Sighing, she went to the sink to rinse out the coffee cup. She wandered through the house trying to find something to keep her mind off Sabrina.

Twenty minutes later, the phone rang.

"Is this Patti Jakowski?"

"Who's this?" she asked.

"I'm Sergeant Carter Caldwell with the Palm Beach Police Department in Florida. Are you the person who called about the young child being left alone?"

"I hope everything turned out all right. Did you find Sabrina?"

A moment's hesitation made Patti's heart drop.

"We did, but we're confused."

Patti's stomach clenched in a knot. "About what?"

"Are you sure you're not her aunt?"

"Of course, I'm sure." The knot tightened. "I would know if she was my niece."

Another long pause.

"Here's the thing. She wasn't dialing your number by mistake. It was programmed into the cell phone. Sabrina's mother taught her to speed dial your number. The house belongs to a..."

"Jamie Jakowski." Patti finished his sentence. Her legs shook, and she reached for the closest chair. She plopped down on the seat. *I should have known. What has Jamie gotten herself into, now?*

"So you do know them?" asked Sergeant Caldwell.

"Jamie's my sister, but I didn't know anything about Sabrina. It's been a long time since Jamie and I talked. Last I knew she lived in New York City, not Florida. And I didn't know she had a daughter." The flush of shame crept up her cheeks. Bad enough having to admit she didn't speak with her sister, but to admit she didn't know she had a niece was worse.

"Well, she's living here, now."

Fury flowed through her. How could her sister leave her child alone like that? Anything could have happened. "So Sabrina was alone." It was a statement, not a question.

"Not exactly."

"What's that mean?"

"Sabrina was confused when she called you. When she went to bed her mom was at home, but when she woke up she wasn't in her bedroom or the house. She panicked and called you, but the nanny was in the house the whole time."

"A nanny?"

How could her sister afford a nanny? The last time she'd seen Jamie she'd been sharing an apartment with roaches.

"The nanny's confused, too. Not sure why Jamie disappeared in the middle of the night. She was scheduled to leave today on a business trip, so she figured your sister couldn't sleep and left early."

Now that was the Jamie she knew. Left without saying goodbye to anyone, and scaring her daughter half-to-death. Apparently, her twin hadn't grown up at all.

"The nanny says they live a quiet life."

"A quiet life? That doesn't sound like Jamie." Anger bubbled up. *Calm down.* Patti tapped her fingers on the telephone and closed her eyes.

Jamie had a child and hadn't told her. That wasn't the kind of news someone forgot to mention. So Jamie must have decided their relationship was over, kaput. Forever.

Deep down, she always thought she and Jamie would one day reconcile. That spark of hope cooled to an ember and then died out completely.

Her bad day had officially turned into a nightmare. "What's going to happen to Sabrina?"

More silence on the other end.

Patti wished she hadn't had the third cup of coffee. Acid churned in her stomach. The caffeine wasn't helping matters, either. Her knees were shaking.

"Nothing. Sabrina's fine. Just a little shook up and wondering why Mom didn't say goodbye to her, but other than that, nothing's amiss."

Patti was wondering the same thing.

"And the nanny's here with the proper documentation proving she's the legal guardian when

Mom is away. So, case closed."

"What about the fact Jamie disappeared in the middle of the night?"

"She's an adult. Her daughter had proper supervision the whole time."

"Has she done this before?"

"I have no idea."

Just leave well enough alone. Sabrina was safe.

The authorities were saying there wasn't a problem.

Her sister and her crazy antics weren't her business, but...Patti could hear Sabrina's sweet little voice. "I want my aunt."

"Maybe, I should come down there and check on Sabrina."

"The nanny is concerned, but at this point it's not a police matter. As I said, Sabrina is fine."

She sighed. "I'm sure Jamie will be back before I could get on a plane. It would just be a wasted trip."

"That's probably true, ma'am. I just wanted to call and let you know the little girl was safe and sound the whole time. And to thank you for taking the time to get involved. A lot of people wouldn't have bothered."

"Thank you for calling me back."

"Do you want the phone number and address?"

She should hang up, and pretend Sabrina had never called her. "What's the number?" she asked.

Patti sat in the chair holding the phone. Despite her twin's many flaws, Patti had a hard time believing Jamie would abandon her child in the middle of the night, no matter what the reason. True, the nanny was there, but to leave without saying goodbye to her child?

Jamie had a daughter.

The thought boggled her mind. Patti chewed the inside of her cheek and then put her head in her hands and cried. Anger surged through her. Her emotions were bouncing faster than a ping-pong ball.

Righteous indignation and compassion for Sabrina, living with a nanny while Jamie went merrily on her way.

Or was she just jealous Jamie had a child and she didn't?

Patti shook away the horrible thought. She wasn't that selfish and self-centered, was she?

Patti's breathing quickened. Not enough air. Trouble breathing. Panic attack. With eyes squeezed shut, she forced herself to slow her breathing down. *One. Two. Three. Four. One. Two. Three.* She didn't want to think about having babies, or her sister.

As soon as her breathing returned to normal, her thoughts returned to Sabrina. Even though Patti and her twin didn't have a relationship, they were still sisters. This little girl was her niece, her family. And Jamie trusted Patti enough to teach Sabrina how to dial her number in an emergency.

And even though it wasn't a real emergency, Sabrina had been terrified, nonetheless.

Thinking of phone numbers, how exactly had Jamie known hers?

Patti hadn't talked with Jamie since she'd moved into her new house, and Patti's number was unlisted so students couldn't find it.

3

Palm Beach, Florida

Patti clenched the arm rests as the plane tilted forward.

The plane hit the runway.

Her head bounced in time with the bumping as they slowed. She looked at her watch. As much as she hated flying, it was still the fastest way to travel. She blew out nervous air.

After several conversations with the nanny, Patti decided she needed to come to Florida.

The nanny had yet to hear from Jamie and was worried.

Sabrina kept crying for her mommy. It was as if the little girl knew something was wrong even if the adults did not.

Patti had no idea how long she'd stay.

Unless Jamie came back home to be with her daughter.

She released the breath she'd been holding, feeling that familiar anger her twin could ignite.

Talk about a love-hate relationship. Her twin could irritate Patti more than any other person on earth. Didn't she understand kids weren't disposable? One couldn't just quit taking care of them when it stopped being fun.

Patti pictured the scene.

Jamie all full of remorse, as always. Apologizing and promising to do better next time. A lot of good that would do. What must her poor niece's life be like with a mother as flighty as Jamie?

That sweet, innocent child deserved better.

If Jamie wasn't capable of taking care of her daughter, Patti was.

Being Sabrina's aunt gave her responsibilities and, unlike Jamie, she wouldn't shirk them. She needed to have a serious talk with her twin about her own responsibilities to her daughter and whether she could fulfill them.

Of course, Jamie had managed to take care of Sabrina for the past four years without any help from her. Jamie may have a legitimate reason for leaving without saying goodbye.

As others stood and jostled Patti, her pulse raced and heat rushed to her face. *I don't have claustrophobia. I don't have claustrophobia. Breathe.*

She forced herself to think about Jamie rather than all the people.

Jamie had a certain sparkle and charm people gravitated towards.

Patti was the quiet one, the awkward one, the one who always felt out of place. She wasn't jealous.

Patti frowned. *Stop lying to yourself.*

That's exactly what it was.

4

Palm trees lined the drive on both sides. Huge beautiful tropical flowers were planted between each tree.

The taxi pulled up to a small sentry building by a gate which protected the exclusive community.

A man stepped from the gatehouse. He bent down and peered into the car.

"Hello, Ms. Jakowski. How are you today? I didn't realize you were out." He looked down at a clipboard and then back up at her. "No record of you leaving. Did something happen to your car?"

Patti was too stunned to reply.

Jamie actually lives in this place. How had her sister managed that?

The guard waited for an answer.

"I'm...I'm not Jamie. I'm her twin sister, Patti. I'm here to visit Sabrina." Patti gulped. "Does...does Jamie travel a lot?"

The guard stared at her open-mouthed, shook his head, and then smiled. "Wow, identical twins, huh?"

She nodded.

"Sure. She travels a lot for work. I know she hates leaving Sabrina so much, but..." The man shrugged. "She's got to pay the bills, right? She'll usually go for a week, or so. Sometimes, she comes back for just a day before she has to leave again."

Perhaps, she'd married a rich man. It had always

been one of Jamie's many lifelong goals. She must have succeeded. *But then again, why not? Everything came so easy to Jamie.* She pushed the angry thoughts away. Right now, she needed to focus on Sabrina, not Jamie. "When was the last time you saw Jamie?"

He walked over to the guard shack and came back holding a paper. "She checked in yesterday about two p.m. and never left again."

How could that be? A second twinge of concern. She'd been so busy assuming Jamie messed up again, she hadn't considered the possibility of a serious problem. In spite of their issues, Patti loved Jamie.

Patti stared out the window as they drove past a private golf course, and then a beautiful clubhouse. Each house sported an immaculate landscaped lawn which abounded with exotic flowers and shrubs. Thinking of her own tiny bungalow in Ohio City she'd worked so hard to buy, she couldn't imagine living in such luxury.

Her stomach twisted.

What had her sister done to afford a house in a place like this?

Jamie had been trying to break into the acting business, but as far as Patti knew, her sister hadn't gotten her big break. Being a waitress didn't pay for these kinds of houses.

The taxi turned into a circular drive leading to a huge house. It reminded her of the plantation from *Gone with the Wind*, including the white marble pillars.

He nodded. "This is it."

5

The door opened before she hit the doorbell.

A stout woman with short, black hair sprinkled with gray, stood before her. "Miss Patti? I'm Anna Martino, Sabrina's nanny. Oh, my. You look just like Miss Jamie. She talks about you mucho. Always showing Sabrina pictures of you and telling her stories about her Aunt Patti."

The revelation surprised Patti to the point of speechlessness. She recovered after a few seconds. "So, have you heard from Jamie, yet?"

Anna's eyes darkened, and her smile faded. "No, something is wrong. She always calls us."

"I understand what you're saying Mrs. Martino, but at this point—"

"*Si, si.* You tell me this already." She smiled at Patti once again. "Sabrina is very excited to meet you. Come in. Come in." Anna led the way. "And please call me Anna."

"I'm excited to meet her as well." Her jaw dropped open as she crossed the threshold.

She said nothing as she looked up at the vaulted cathedral ceiling and the loft. The living room was done all in white, white sofas, white carpet, white coffee tables, and white walls. Elegant was the only word to describe it. Judging from the outside, she'd expected a beautiful house, but she wasn't prepared for the opulence.

Patti scrimped and saved every penny to buy her little house, but it was a shack compared to this place.

She looked at the marble stands, the white leather furniture, and the snow-white rug that adorned the sitting area in front of the marble-white fireplace.

Her gaze moved upwards to the picture hanging above the fireplace, the only color in the room.

It showed a stylized figure of girl staring at her reflection in the mirror. Instead of the reflection being the same, it showed the same face, but with a darker feel. The girl was reaching through the mirror as if to hug her reflection or to pull her into the darkness of her own world.

Patti walked over to examine the picture more closely. She looked at the signature.

A Picasso!

The painting wasn't the real thing, was it? Considering the quality of the rest of the house, it very well could be.

Anna motioned for her to sit. "I will go get Sabrina so she can finally meet her *tia*."

I have nothing to feel guilty about. Jamie was the one who broke the ties. Jamie was the one who ruined Patti's chance at happiness. Jamie was the one who chose to stop coming home to Ohio. If Jamie had ever bothered to come back, they might have fixed their fractured relationship.

Anna walked back in holding Sabrina's hand. A beautiful child. Her shiny black hair was chin length and straight, her forehead covered by bangs. With beautiful olive-colored skin and dark eyes surrounded by thick dark eyelashes, it was obvious she hadn't inherited Patti and Jamie's pale coloring.

Her niece.

Her eyes filled with tears. "Hi." Patti smiled.

Instead of answering, Sabrina's arm encircled Anna's one leg. She hid her face.

Anna shrugged. "She's shy sometimes." She lowered her voice. "And she have trouble with making all her sounds. She goes to speech therapy two times every week."

Patti nodded in understanding, remembering Sabrina's phone call and the problems they had communicating.

Anna pulled her away from her leg. "Mi poquita, say hello to Tia Patti."

One eye peeked out at her. Without warning Sabrina ran over and stared at Patti. "You wook wike Mommy."

Patti smiled at her niece. "You're right, honey. I do look like your mommy, but I'm your Aunt Patti. Remember? We talked on the phone."

"Aunt Patti?" Sabrina yelled as if just making the connection.

"That's me, sweetie." Patti reached her arms out to the little girl, who tumbled into them.

Sabrina snuggled into Patti. The four-year-old smelled of grape soda. She felt warm and loveable as she clung to Patti.

Patti's heart melted.

"I can only stay a few days."

Sabrina looked at Patti. Her mouth trembled and her eyes filled with tears. "You mad at me, Aunt Patti?" Her lips puckered.

Patti patted her arm."No, honey. I'm not mad at you. It's just...."

"Then why can't you stay?"Anna asked.

She didn't have a good answer. School was

finished for the summer, and her time was her own to do as she wished. It seemed selfish of her not to want to help out her adorable niece, but she didn't deal well with the unexpected.

And this situation was very much unexpected.

"It's just that...I don't know...I'm sure Jamie will be back long before Monday. This is just like Jamie to—" Patti stopped mid-sentence and looked around the house.

None of this seemed like Jamie in the least. Jamie with a mansion. Jamie with a daughter.

She shook her head not knowing how to finish the sentence.

Anna and Patti sat in the middle of the stark white living room staring at each other, neither knowing what to say or do.

Finally, Patti broke the silence. "I guess the best thing is to follow Sabrina's usual schedule. That will make her less anxious."

"Oh, she's not anxious. Miss Jamie is gone mucho with her work. Sabrina is used to her mommy being gone, aren't you, poquita?"Anna hugged Sabrina close to her.

Sabrina nodded as she wiggled out of Anna's arms. Anna focused her attention on Sabrina as if Patti weren't there.

"Well, well, Miss Sabrina. What do you want now?"

"I want to play."

"OK, then. We go to your playroom."

Sabrina and Anna walked towards a closed door.

Anna looked back at Patti. "You can come."

Patti followed them down a marble tiled hallway to another door.

Anna opened the door and Sabrina ran through the doorway.

It was larger than Patti's living room and kitchen combined. Two purple overstuffed sofas formed an *L* shape. Orange and white pillows littered the sofa and the floor. Lots of windows and a sliding door made up one wall to let in the afternoon sun. Huge modern art hung on the walls, also in shades of purple and orange. Toys were scattered across the floor, and a large flat screen TV hung on the wall.

This room felt like more like Jamie.

Overflowing bookcases lined the wall. Jamie loved to read as much as Patti. It was one of their few common interests. They'd often read the same book, and then discussed it into the wee hours of the morning.

Patti's eyes teared up at the memory. Funny how she'd forgotten that.

Sabrina ran to the toy chest and grabbed a baby doll.

"Miss Sabrina," Anna called to her in a stern voice, but she glanced at Patti with a smile.

Patti had a feeling Sabrina had Anna wrapped around her little finger.

"This room is a mess. You need to put your toys away before you can play."

Sabrina looked at Anna as if deciding whether to push her, or not. "Otay." Sabrina sat the doll back in its crib and began picking up the toys and placing them in the toy boxes.

Anna turned toward Patti. "Miss Jamie very strict. She always make her clean up before letting her play again. Of course, the room will be a mess again before you know it, but it is a rule."

Patti motioned around the room. "This looks much more like Jamie than out there."

"She spend most time here. Other room just for show."

Patti stepped closer. "Anna, why would she leave in the middle of the night without telling you?"

Anna's eyes darkened and a troubled look crossed her face. She walked over and sat on the couch. Patti followed. "Miss Jamie would never do that. She adore Sabrina. *Ella es una madre muy buena.* Miss Jamie would never leave without telling her goodbye. We have a routine."

Patti's stomach flip-flopped at the conviction in Anna's voice. "What's that?"

"They give each other kisses and more kisses. Then, Miss Jamie take Sabrina's picture with her cell phone, and Sabrina take her Mommy's picture with mine. More kisses and hugs, and then Miss Jamie leave, but she calls her two or three times as she is traveling to the airport."

"Then what do you think happened?"

Anna shook her head. "I don't know. Miss Jamie would never leave Sabrina without saying *adios*, unless..."

"Unless? Unless what, Anna?" Her voice grew urgent. "If you have an idea what might have happened, you need to tell me."

Anna shook her head. "All I was going to say is something bad must have happened."

"Do you know anything about her job? Where she works or why she travels so much? Anything. If we knew, we might be able to track her down."

Anna looked at Patti for several long moments as if trying to decide how much she should trust this stranger. Finally, as if she'd come to a decision, she nodded. "She not really work much the first few years we live here, and she didn't travel, but then she start to travel some. About a year ago, she began to travel *mucho*."

"What did she tell you about the travel?"

"She not talk about it. I know when she get home from trips, she acted nervous and upset. Sometime, I hear her crying at night during her dreams. After a few days, she would calm down and be OK." Anna sighed and twisted her hands. "Until she would leave again."

Nightmares had always been a problem for Jamie, especially during times of stress.

"How long have you worked for her?"

"I moved in with her when she pregnant. I drove Miss Jamie to the hospital. I was her Lamaze coach." Anna said, naming a popular birthing process.

More guilt, but Patti refused to accept it. She hadn't known Jamie was pregnant. She'd have helped. A little voice in her head asked if she was sure about that. She ignored the voice. "Do you know anything about Sabrina's father?"

Anna shook her head. "These are things she won't talk about. When I try, she either gets sad, or mad, so I stop asking."

"What *does* she talk about?" Patti asked as she picked up a tiny orange pillow off the sofa and hugged it to herself. She needed to learn more about Jamie's life with Anna and Sabrina.

Something was wrong.

It wasn't like Jamie to be secretive. If anything, Jamie was the opposite. She had loved to tell everyone about everything, always assuming everyone wanted to know about the minutia of her life.

"Lately, she's been talking about moving home. She said soon we would live in Ohio."

"Really?" Patti's mouth dropped open.

She hadn't talked with Jamie in almost seven years. The last thing she expected was her sister to have a child, and then desert her. They hadn't been raised in such a way. Her worry moved up another notch and was close to becoming anxiety.

Patti turned to Anna. "Did she say why she couldn't move back right now?"

"Just the job was not over, but soon it would be finished and she could go home. She would smile when she talked about going home, about you. She loves you *mucho*. Miss Jamie didn't smile much lately."

The rocks in Patti's stomach grew larger.

"She want me to go with them, but I don't know. Not after I hear her tell Sabrina about the snow and the winters. They sound very bad."

"They can get nasty."

"Where is your luggage? Your things? I will take them up to the guest room."

"The airlines lost it. From now on, I'll only take carry-on luggage. I guess I better go shopping."

Anna tapped her chin and frowned. "Not necessary. You look same size as Miss Jamie so you can wear her clothes. She not mind. Very nice of you to fly down to help Sabrina. God bless you, such a good woman."

Patti bit her lip, shamed by Anna's words. She didn't feel like a good woman, and she was sure God hadn't been pleased with her attitude when she'd first learned about Sabrina.

She'd come down out of guilt, not love. But now that she was here, she was so glad she'd made the right decision. "I didn't know I had a niece. Did Jamie tell you why she never told me about Sabrina?"

"She say you very busy. No need her interrupting your life."

Patti stared at Anna.

Why would Jamie say such a thing? Jamie knew she'd never be too busy to spend time with her niece, no matter what the situation between the two of them.

Something was wrong.

Patti bit her lip and moved over to where Sabrina sat in front of a huge Victorian-style doll house. It was obvious Jamie had spared no money when she'd purchased it. It was as elegant as the house she stood in at the moment.

Sabrina looked up at Patti. "Want to play with me?"

"I do." She eased herself down on the floor, wishing she were a bit more limber. She needed to get back to exercising regularly.

6

Patti sat on the most comfortable sofa she'd ever experienced. Money might not be able to buy love, but it sure could buy comfort.

Across the room, Sabrina still played with the huge doll house, oblivious to the adults in the room.

Anna had to know more about Jamie's comings and goings.

"Jamie may have told you not to talk about her private concerns, but I think this constitutes an emergency."

Instead of answering, Anna turned on the baby monitor sitting on the coffee table and stood. "I take you up to your room. You must be very tired."

Anna walked over to Sabrina. "I be back in a few minutes, sweet baby. Then, we make dinner and eat."

"I'm not a baby. I'm a big girl. Aunt Patti said so." Sabrina waved goodbye to Patti and moved to the rocking chair with her baby doll.

Anna led the way down the hall. At the end of the hall, she pointed at a door. "This is the guest room, you can sleep there. Jamie is your sister. You go in her room, borrow clothes, do whatever you want."

"Thanks, Anna." Patti patted Anna's shoulder. "I know you must be worried, but Jamie has always been irresponsible. I'm sure she's fine."

Anna looked at Patti with sorrow in her eyes. "No, she is not fine. Miss Jamie never leave Sabrina like this.

And she would always call once a day when she was gone, sometimes two times in a day. Something is very wrong." Anna's lips thinned. "Miss Jamie is not irresponsible. It has been a long time since you see her. You do not know Miss Jamie, now."

Patti's stomach clenched. She didn't want to acknowledge the truth in Anna's words, but she was right. She had no idea what kind of mother Jamie was. Who was she to make the judgment Jamie was a bad mother?

Patti fought the overwhelming urge to explain to Anna it wasn't her fault.

Jamie was the one who betrayed Patti, not the other way around. Her twin walked out of her life.

Instead, she agreed with her sister's biggest fan. "I suppose you're right, Anna."

Anna nodded, satisfied, and scurried back to Sabrina.

Patti stood in front of the guestroom, but instead of entering, she went back to Jamie's room. For several seconds she stood there, feeling the need to knock, but knew it was ridiculous. She opened the door and walked inside.

The room had a homey feel to it, unlike the living room downstairs. The furniture, including the bed, was a simple California Mission style with a rich oak color. The soft green wallpaper was complimented by pink curtains and carpet. There were tons of pillows on the unmade bed.

Other than the bed, the room was spotless.

Patti smiled and shook her head as she stared at the unmade mess.

Jamie hadn't changed much.

Their mother forced them countless times to make

their bed.

Jamie argued it made no sense when it would get messed up again that very night.

Patti stood in the middle of the room, not sure what to do. Maybe she could find a clue as to her sister's whereabouts.

The computer was a logical place to start, so she walked over to the desk in the corner and booted up. While waiting for the computer, Patti rummaged through the drawers. She found the expected stamps, pens, paper clips and other such items, but nothing personal.

No address book. No pay stubs. Nothing to tell Patti where Jamie worked, or who her friends were. However, she did find a checkbook.

Patti opened the cover, and then closed it. It felt like a violation of privacy. She fingered the embossed initials and then flipped it open once again.

Patti blinked at the numbers.

Wow. What could Jamie be doing to make that kind of money?

She set it aside and continued her search. In the third drawer Patti opened, she hit the jackpot. It was stuffed full of papers. Hopefully, she'd could find a clue to Jamie's job in the mess.

Patti pulled out the papers and put them in piles. Some were health insurance statements, while others were old bills and an assortment of documents. She came across statements from a stock company.

She shuffled through the papers until she found the most recent statement. Patti shook her head and stared at the numbers.

Her sister was a wealthy woman.

Her own savings account barely contained three

thousand and she didn't own any stocks.

Ashamed, she shrugged off the jealousy and focused on Jamie.

Among the statements was a piece of paper with a user name and password written on it.

Patti snorted.

The password was "Sabrina." How obvious.

Patti hit the keys and within seconds, she was logged in. She looked through the document files. Having found nothing of interest in them, she searched through every file on the hard drive, but again, she found nothing to help her find Jamie.

She walked over to the closet and stuck her head in. Not a closet, but more like a dressing room. It was huge, but mostly empty. One side held shelves for shoes and purses. Most were sneakers and simple sandals with a few dressier pairs. On the opposite side hung Jamie's clothes.

Curiosity got the best of her. Patti browsed through them. Again, nothing fancy. Considering the mansion Patti stood in, Jamie's clothes weren't what she expected.

She walked over to boxes sitting on the far side of the walk-in. She looked through each of the boxes and was disappointed to find nothing.

She turned to leave, but her gaze fell on a purse thrown haphazardly in the far corner.

Her stomach clenched.

Women didn't leave their purses—for any reason. She'd heard of women running back into burning buildings to get them.

Maybe Jamie was using a different one at the moment, Patti reasoned, trying to reassure herself.

Patti opened the Gucci handbag. Just the usual

things: a brush, makeup, some gum.

She opened the billfold. Her breath faltered. Inside were several credit cards and a driver's license. The license showed the address of the house Patti was sitting in at the moment.

It was Jamie's current purse.

Patti's concern moved up several notches from mild anxiety to apprehension.

Why would Jamie walk out of the house without her purse or her child? She stared down at the license, barely able to breathe.

Her heart reached out to Jamie's.

Where are you, sis? Are you in trouble?

Nothing. No answers. No connection with her twin. Tears dripped on the license she still held. It didn't matter. She knew the answer.

Jamie hadn't left this house willingly.

7

After Patti pulled herself together, she went to her own purse for the number the policeman had given her. What was his name? She found the note.

Carter Caldwell, Sergeant.

She would not wait until Monday morning to file a missing person report. She didn't care about the rules. It was crucial Jamie be treated as a missing person now. Every minute her sister was gone, made it less likely...

She shook the thoughts away.

No, I refuse to think like that. Not going to do it. Only positive thoughts.

She pulled out her cell phone out and hit the numbers, hoping he'd be reasonable.

"Caldwell here."

"Sergeant Caldwell, this is Patti Jakowski, Sabrina's au—"

"Did your sister come back, or have you heard from her?"

"No, she didn't come back. I was calling because I found her purse."

"And?"

Patti felt foolish. *Why had she ever thought a man would understand?* "Women never leave the house without their purse. They just don't do that. S...s...something must have happened. It just doesn't make sense."

There was silence on the other end. "I see what you're getting at, but I hardly think finding her purse indicates foul play."

"If Jamie was on some business trip somewhere, she would need her ID. I...I don't think she planned on leaving."

There was a long silence. Finally he spoke. "I'm on my way, I'll be there in fifteen minutes."

The detective hung up before Patti could tell him he needed to file a missing person report.

She rummaged through Jamie's closet and picked out a simple sundress to wear.

Patti went to the guest room and looked in the mirror. Her eyes were red and swollen and her hair was a mess. She felt dirty and grimy from the airplane ride. She peeled off her clothes and jumped in the shower.

Anna knocked on the door. "The policeman is here. He said you called him."

"Thanks, Anna."

Patti picked up her own purse, as well as Jamie's.

Anna waited for Patti outside the door. "Sabrina is ready for bed. Would you like to say goodnight before she falls asleep?"

Patti nodded.

Anna smiled at her. "I will be in my own room if you need me."

"OK. Can you tell Detective Caldwell I'll be down after I tuck Sabrina in?"

Anna nodded and walked away.

Patti couldn't decide if the woman was upset at her for calling the detective. Probably not. It was an awkward situation for both of them.

Patti walked into Sabrina's room. It was a room fit

for a princess. It was all pink and lacy with a canopy bed. The walls had a continuous mural that extended to all four of them, with castles, a pretty garden, and princesses. A little girl's dream of what a bedroom should be.

Jamie had made sure Sabrina had the luxuries their parents hadn't been able to give them.

Sabrina was propped up on the bed amid a mountain of pillows with her thumb in her mouth.

"Hi, sweetie. Are you ready to go to bed?"

The little girl nodded but said nothing. Her dark brown gaze followed Patti's movements.

"It's been a long day, huh."

Sabrina removed her thumb. "Where's mommy? Her didn't say goodbye."

Out of the mouth of babes.

"I don't know where she is, but you're not to worry about it, OK? Your mommy loves you."

Another tiny nod, but tears pooled in Sabrina's chocolate brown eyes.

Patti leaned down and hugged her niece. Her own worry moved up another notch. "Now are you ready for a story?"

A little smile.

After Patti read two stories, Sabrina's little eyes fluttered closed and she slept.

Patti removed the little girl's thumb from her mouth and left the room.

She walked down the winding staircase.

In the snowy-white living room, a man stood in front of the Picasso staring intently at it. He looked over at her. "Is it real?"

Patti examined the stylized picture of a woman looking in the mirror at a reflection. It was eerie the way it reminded her of Jamie and her. They looked the same on the outside, but not the inside.

"I don't know a thing about art." She turned away. The painting disturbed her for some reason. "I'm Patti Jakowski, by the way."

He turned towards her with a smile as sunny as a Florida afternoon pasted on his handsome face.

Carter Caldwell looked more like an actor playing a cop than a cop, handsome and rugged. And it was hard to miss his muscles in his tight-fitting blue polo shirt.

She glanced at his left hand. No ring. When she looked up he was watching her with intense green eyes. Her face grew warm as he grinned at her.

"So, this is quite the place, isn't it?" He ran a hand over the marble mantle.

"Not exactly what I pictured for Jamie's house when you called."

"So, she didn't buy it with old family money?"

The last time Patti saw Jamie, she'd been trying to break into the acting business. Being a waitress at a bar on Broadway didn't pay for these kinds of houses.

"Hardly. Our parents died when we were teenagers and any money they left us was long gone before I graduated from college."

Jamie had gone to college, but quit. One more thing she hadn't seen through to the end.

"According to the nanny, she's not married, so she didn't get rich that way. Any ideas how she can afford this lifestyle?"

Patti stared at the man. Could she trust him? Should she tell him what she'd found in Jamie's room? She made her decision. "I was looking around Jamie's room, and I found a checkbook and some other financial accounts. If those accounts are any indication, it could be an original." She pointed at the Picasso.

She paused, not wanting to ask the next question. "Are you thinking she might have made her money illegally?"

"Let's not jump to conclusions, yet. We really don't know anything at this point."

She sat on the white leather sofa.

He sat in a chair opposite her.

Patti held up Jamie's purse. "Something's wrong. I know you believe it's silly, but women don't leave their purses behind willingly. And how can she be on a business trip without money, or ID, or credit cards. It doesn't make sense. As far as I'm conc—"

"The police need a little more to file a missing person report than a purse that was left behind. After all, she's an adult and—"

"The nanny insists Jamie would never leave Sabrina without saying goodbye. The security guards have no record of her leaving." Patti took a breath and groped for her next words. "Someone must...must have made her leave. It's the only explanation."

"I can think of others." He shrugged.

"What's that supposed to mean?"

"Your sister pays Anna's wages. What else would you expect her to say? Of course, she's going to defend her employer."

She felt warm anger creeping up her neck. She opened her mouth. "You can't just ignore the fact she seems to have disappeared into thin air."

"I'm not ignoring it, really, I'm not. I know this is a tough situation, but waiting is always the hardest part. She'll probably show up sometime tonight with a logical explanation of where she was."

"So, you aren't going to do anything about it?" Her eyes challenged him.

"I didn't say that." His green gaze was serious. "I'll go back to the station and do some checking."

☙❧

Carter went into his office at the police station, and tripped over two books he'd forgotten to pick up earlier. He retrieved them and walked towards the bookshelf, but stopped. No room there. He had to get this place more organized, if he could only find the time.

He stacked the books on a pile of reports that also needed filing. The books slid off the pile, taking several reports with them. He shook his head. What a slob he'd become. He was sure a psychologist could explain this new behavior.

Not that it took a genius to figure it out.

With a sigh, Carter opened the computer file. Enough time may not have elapsed for a missing person report, but it didn't mean he couldn't do a little preliminary research.

Something felt wrong about the way Jamie Jakowski disappeared in the middle of the night—without her purse or cell phone.

Of course, there could be any number of explanations, but his mind kept thinking of the worst ones.

An old boyfriend, even Sabrina's father, could have come back with revenge on his mind and kidnapped her.

Drugs or alcohol could be another reason.

Jamie might be an addict. She wouldn't be the first

addict to abandon a child.

Maybe, she'd been on the wagon, but as he knew too well from his days in the vice squad, once an addict always an addict.

Perhaps, the pressure of being a single mother was too much for Jamie Jakowski, and she'd succumbed to an old demon.

As Carter finished filling the name and address into the missing person report, he wondered what the story was between the sisters. Twins were supposed to be close. Patti Jakowski hadn't even known her niece existed.

He thought of Patti and her turquoise-blue eyes. He was attracted to her, but he wasn't looking for a relationship. He didn't need the aggravation or the pain. Besides, any woman would have to be crazy to get involved with a cop.

His thoughts went to the two sisters. Families shouldn't stay angry at each other. Life was too short for such nonsense. One never knew when something bad would happen, and then it would be too late to repair the relationship.

He clicked the mouse on his computer. He typed in Jamie Jakowski's name and hit the enter button. In seconds, the database came up.

Carter's heart sank.

Jamie had been arrested a number of times, but only on misdemeanors. The charges showed a definite drug connection. No felony charges, but it didn't mean this woman wasn't involved in the drug business in a big way. That could explain a lot, including her million-dollar house and why she happened to be missing.

Carter sighed. Time to ask Patti some hard

questions.

⁂

Patti paced around Jamie's kitchen. It was hard not to compare the ultra-modern, ultra-expensive kitchen to her tiny one back in Ohio.

Her nerves jangled, there was no way she'd be able to sleep. She picked up Jamie's keys.

Anna told her she'd need the key card to get back in the gate leading out to the beach.

She opened the door, surprised at the warmth.

Turn left on the road in front of the house and it would lead to the beach. Those were Anna's instructions when she'd asked.

Her footsteps slowed when she heard a car behind her.

Sgt. Caldwell, with his charming smile and twinkling green eyes, stepped out of the SUV. He waved and jogged towards her. He gave her another charming smile, but his tone was serious. "We need to talk."

Patti's stomach clenched. "I was taking a walk to calm my nerves."

"Sounds like a plan."

The beach was less than ten minutes from Jamie's house.

They didn't speak during the walk. As they reached the entrance to the beach, the gate stood open allowing anyone to walk in.

Patti looked at Carter. "So much for security."

Carter looked grim. "Looks like anyone can come and go as they please."

After they walked through, Patti closed the gate

making sure the lock snapped in place. Patti turned to Carter. "Okay, tell me what you need to tell me about Jamie. Let's just get it over."

His cell phone rang. "Hold on a minute. I need to answer this." He walked several steps away. Within minutes, he snapped the phone shut. "Sorry about that."

"Not a problem. Tell me—"

"I need a few minutes to check on something." He pointed to some wooden beach chairs lined up against the brick wall. "I'll be back in a minute. Sit down and enjoy the view."

Before Patti could protest, Carter hiked up the beach and away from her.

She couldn't relax. She paced in front of the row of chairs, and then sat down.

The moon was a full ball of light. It glimmered on the ripples of the ocean's waves.

She slipped off her sandals and dug her toes into the sand, still warm from the heat of the day.

The gentle rolling of the ocean waves gradually mesmerized her and tension oozed out. She closed her eyes and listened to the whooshing sounds. When she opened them, she watched the never-ending waves, and knew God was in control. He was more than able to handle whatever problems life handed her.

"Nice view, huh?"

She jumped, and then smiled to cover her embarrassment.

"Sorry, I didn't mean to scare you," he said, taking a seat beside her.

"I was watching the waves...and...and thinking." She ducked her head to hide the tears.

"Why don't you and your sister keep in contact?"

he asked, pinning her with a look. "I always imagined twins to be super close."

Patti squirmed. "I guess most twins are, but we haven't been close since we graduated from high school. We sort of went our own separate ways."

"Why are you mad at her?"

"What makes you think I'm mad at her?"

"Are you kidding? You were so mad on the phone I thought I was going to have to fly to Ohio to calm you down."

She reached down and picked up a handful of sand, and then watched as it slipped through her fingers. She glanced up at Carter. "That's not true. I was a little shocked. I hadn't heard from Jamie in years, and besides, I was upset over Sabrina being left alone."

He shook his head. "No way. I'm not buying it. It was much more than that. I know when someone is mad."

I don't see what that ha—"

"I need to understand Jamie better before I know what direction to take with this investigation. Whatever you and Anna can tell me about her will help."

She took a deep breath and felt the old familiar pain. "She came home for my wedding, but thanks to her, the wedding never happened."

"Why not?"

She attempted a lighter tone. "You ask tough questions, Officer Caldwell."

"Just doing my job, ma'am. So?"

Why couldn't she get over it? "Things didn't work out."

"Mmm."

Her face felt warm. From embarrassment, shame, or anger? Probably all three. Her gaze strayed back to the ocean. She cleared her throat, hoping she could keep the emotion out of her voice. "Jamie came home a few weeks before the wedding. My fiancé went gaga over Jamie the minute he met her. She kept telling me he wasn't right for me, but I didn't want to listen. Jamie flirted with him outrageously. At one point, I overheard him talking to Jamie. He was asking her to..."

Patti stopped. She didn't want to remember the conversation. She'd heard it in her mind for the past seven years. "You can imagine what it was. It was ugly, and it made me realize he wasn't the man I wanted to marry."

"And you felt Jamie was to blame."

Patti wiped away tears. "Wouldn't you?"

"I can understand why you'd be upset." Sgt. Caldwell said in a non-committal tone. "But did you ever consider she might have been protecting you from a man who wasn't going to be honest with you? That maybe she didn't really want him, but was trying to show you what kind of man he was?"

Patti's heart cracked.

Jamie wouldn't have done that...would she?

She thought back to the ugly scene with her fiancé and sister. Everything she'd wanted in life was destroyed that day.

No husband.

No children.

Patti had dreamed of a family. And it was gone in an instant. This man didn't understand.

"I was led to believe forgiveness was what that cross you're wearing is all about." He pointed at her necklace. "Of course, it doesn't happen overnight. Forgiving someone can take a long time," His voice was gentle.

Shame burned. "It is." The tears were falling harder. *I'm a failure. As a sister, an aunt, but mostly as a Christian.*

Patti looked out at the ocean for a few moments as she worked to gain control of her emotions. Glancing back at the detective, she wondered about the sadness she heard in his voice.

It sounded as if he'd had his share of learning how to forgive.

She wiped at the tears and looked at him. "I'm such a mess."

"We all are. That's why it's a wonderful thing God's mercies are new each morning."

Patti considered his words. "I suppose, but I've got such a bad feeling."

"I could tell you everything will be fine, but –"

"I know," Patti said. A wave washed into the shore. "I'd rather you be honest, than try to make me feel better."

"That's a deal I can live with." Carter hesitated, then turned to her as though this was the moment of truth. "Was Jamie ever into drugs?"

It took a moment for her to grasp the meaning of his question. "No, of course not. What a ridiculous question. What would make you thi—"

"I just –"

"You're wrong. Jamie wouldn't do something like that."

"Think about it, Patti. She has a lot of money and lives a lavish lifestyle. Her nanny doesn't know what she does for a living and claims she can't call her when she's away. What does it sound like to you?"

"I admit it doesn't sound good, but I can't believe she would sell drugs." Her heart pounded and bile rose up in her throat.

Jamie selling drugs?

The thought sickened her.

"Was she *ever* into drugs?" he asked in a more gentle tone.

"For awhile, but nothing serious. She certainly wasn't selling them."

"I checked her arrest record, earlier."

Patti waited for the other shoe to drop.

Jamie, arrested?

"She's been arrested before."

"If you already knew that, why play this game with me?" Anger tinged her voice.

"Because it's not clear-cut, and I wanted to hear what you said, first. No felonies, just some misdemeanors."

"Did they have to do with drugs?" Patti asked as she sat back down in a chair.

"Some did and some didn't."

Her stomach clenched. "Some. How many times was she arrested?"

"Eight," Carter said.

"Eight times. Jamie's been arrested eight times?" Patti rubbed a hand against her forehead. "I had no idea. I can't believe this."

She couldn't handle any more. Patti jumped from her chair.

Sgt. Caldwell followed suit, but she held a hand up.

"I need some time alone."

8

Carter stared after her as she walked down the beach.

His brain said not to get emotionally involved with this beautiful woman from Ohio, but his heart told him otherwise. It had been a long time since he'd felt this attracted to someone.

When his wife, Nancy, died, he'd vowed to never remarry. Still, he could visualize Patti's lips and...

A noise in the dark drew Carter's attention.

A jogger. The man stopped running and stared at the closed gate. The jogger turned and his eyes widened as he noticed Carter. "Hey, didn't see you sitting there."

Carter went into full cop mode. "You live in there?" he asked.

"I wish." The jogger chuckled. "Just stopping to dream about the day when I can afford it. How about you—you live there?"

"Nah, just taking a break. Enjoying the view."

"Gotta get going. Don't want the muscles to cool down. Have a good one." The man turned and ran.

The hairs on the back of Carter's neck tingled. *A harmless jogger. That's all the man was. No reason to be worried.*

As Carter glanced down the beach, he saw Patti.

The man was jogging towards Patti...Ms. Jakowski.

Carter started a slow jog in the same direction. Too

slow. He picked up his speed.

Another shadowed figure walked towards him and the jogger. Patti must have turned around.

Carter increased his speed. Too far away. He ran harder. "Hey, Patti. I got tired of waiting for you," he called.

The jogger sprinted past Patti and into the darkness.

∂∞ঙ

Patti stood rooted to the spot. Her heart lurched as she watched the bizarre chase scene.

The man ran towards her, but when Sgt. Caldwell yelled, the jogger veered away.

As he passed she saw anger and hatred in his face.

A moment later Sgt. Caldwell was by her side.

"What's wrong?" Patti's own heart raced, though she had no idea why. "Who was that man? Why were you chasing him?"

Sgt Caldwell sucked in air. "Are you OK? Did he say or do anything to you?"

"What made you think I wasn't OK? Why were you chasing him?"

"It can be scary out on the beach in the dark. I didn't want him to scare you. Did you get a look at him?"

"No, but he looked so angry when he ran past me. Do you think he had something to do with Jamie?"

"Not really. Just the cop in me being suspicious." He took a few deep breaths. "I need to start spending more time in the gym. I'm getting out of shape."

"It doesn't look that way to me." She realized how that sounded. "I mean you look good to...I mean...never mind what I mean."

Sgt Caldwell chuckled.

"I didn't mean it like that, Sgt. Caldwell."

"Call me Carter. And whatever you say, Ms. Jakowski."

He'd chased the man because he thought she might be frightened. She touched his arm for a quick second. "Thanks for worrying about me."

"Not a problem."

They started back towards the gate.

"I hate to bring this up, but we need to finish our conversation."

"I know. Sorry I ran away."

"You didn't really run away, you left for a few minutes," Carter said.

"What makes you think I was coming back?"

His lips quirked.

"To answer your question." Patti decided to get the conversation back on track. "As far as I know, Jamie's never been into serious drinking, or doing drugs, but I haven't seen her in more than seven years, so that could have changed. But it's hard for me to imagine her dealing drugs under any circumstances."

"I know you don't want to hear it, but it makes sense. It could explain the money she's made in a relatively short amount of time."

"I know."

"Any other ideas how she made her money?"

"Well, she was trying to break into acting. Maybe she succeeded?" It sounded lame.

"I'll see what I can find out. I have a friend who's a whiz at computers. I'll ask him to check into her finances. Maybe he can figure out where the money comes from."

"Thanks, Sergeant." She moved to the gate leading to Jamie's housing development. She slid in the key card and waited for the buzz to let them in.

"Let's get you home."

She swayed ever so slightly, emotionally drained and physically tired.

"You must be exhausted after the day you've had." He said sympathetically. He reached out and steadied her.

Instead of shrugging him off, she leaned against him for just a moment, savoring the warmth. Embarrassed, she stepped back, mentally promising not be taken in by his sweetness, charm, or good looks.

That had happened once before, and she vowed never again.

9

"Lock the doors and make sure the security system is engaged." Carter instructed.

"Yes, sir." Her irritation was evident.

He waited until she shut the door and he heard the lock click in place, then he moved to his car with purpose.

The jogger on the beach worried him a great deal more than he'd let on to Patti. Of course, he might not have anything to do with Jamie's disappearance, but at this point Carter wasn't taking any chances.

After his wife's death he'd always chosen to go beyond reasonable duty when it came to others' safety. If he could prevent others from the pain he'd suffered, he'd do whatever he could. Since becoming a Christian, he knew this was a God-given responsibility, and one he gladly accepted.

He pulled his car up to the gatehouse.

The security guard leaned back in the chair, head nodding.

Carter walked up to the shack. *So much for top-notch security.* He rapped on the window—hard.

The guard jerked awake and glared at him.

Carter flashed his badge.

The man slid open the window. "Yes, Officer, what can I do for you?"

"We've got a problem. Well, actually you have a problem. Do you have any idea how easy it is for someone to get through the beach gate?"

The security guard rubbed his eyes and stared at Carter for a moment. He nodded. "Yeah, but management doesn't want to do anything about it. Afraid it would make people uncomfortable, and too curious about what was behind the brick wall. We've got security cameras mounted." The guard pointed to the monitors behind him. "Look at that. One of the cameras is broken again."

Carter stared at the blank monitor screen. His mind flashed to the camera sitting so prominently on the fence. "From the beach area?"

The man's eyes widened. "Yeah, how'd you know?"

"Was it working earlier?"

It wouldn't take anything but a thrown rock to break the camera. Then the jogger, or anyone else, could waltz into the development undetected.

His blood pumped faster. He needed to get back to Jamie's house.

Before someone else did.

"Yeah, a few minutes ago. The last time I checked."

"Are there cameras set up on the grounds as well?"

Maybe they had footage that could show Jamie leaving—if she left on her own.

He needed to get back to the house.

"Just a few, like on the golf course and at the clubhouse. We don't have them set up to view the homes. That would be an invasion of privacy."

"Too bad."

"Is that all you wanted to tell me?"

"We've got a problem at the Jakowski property,

and I need you to put surveillance on it for the night. I want someone in front and in back of the property. We need to make sure no one breaks in there tonight."

The man's eyes bulged and then he shook his head. "I can't do that."

"Look, there's a very real possibility that Jamie Jakowski disappeared from her house in the middle of the night. Do you want to be responsible for her daughter and sister disappearing, too?"

The man's eyes bugged out even more. "No, but there's me and one other guy. I can't leave here. I'm not allowed to. I—"

"Fine, get the other guy to sit in front of the Jakowski house. Make sure he's in plain sight, and I'll take the back of the house. Does that work for you?"

"Sure. He's on a golf cart patrolling the grounds."

"Perfect. Tell him to go to the front of the house, and stay parked there until daylight. Tell him to stay in full view so people can see him and know the house is being watched."

Carter drove up and parked in front of Jamie's house. He walked around the back, making sure no windows or doors were open and accessible. By the time he was on the second trip around the house, the security guard on the golf cart arrived.

The guard didn't look to be twenty. He was skinny and wore glasses. He ran hands through his stringy black hair. "Do...do...do you think there's going to be a problem?"

"Not if I can help it."

"But...but...I haven't got a weap—"

"You don't need one. I have one if there's a problem, but we're here to make sure there isn't a problem. Being visible should stop anything from happening."

The boy's Adam's apple bobbed for a moment. "Are you sure?"

"No, I'm not sure, but I'm praying that's what will happen. Stay out here and don't leave. Got it?"

"Got it."

"And stay awake. I'll be around back." Carter stared down at the golf cart. "Does that thing have a horn?"

The boy nodded.

"Good. Honk if you need me." Carter went to the back patio. The lights were off inside. Good.

Patti needed to get some sleep. She'd barely had the energy to walk back.

Restless, he marched back and forth, being careful not to make any noise. After his adrenaline had calmed, he sat at the patio table. He'd spend the night and sneak off in the morning.

With luck, Patti and Anna would never know they'd been guarded throughout the night.

No reason to alarm them.

Chances were, they weren't in any danger.

☙❧

Patti wandered from room to room in the darkened house trying to reconnect with her sister. There was an eerie hush throughout the rooms, as if they mourned the loss of their owner.

Patti pushed away the negative thought. She wouldn't give up on Jamie. She sat down on the leather sofa and stared at the spotlighted Picasso.

Looking at the girl reaching through the mirror, it was as if Jamie was trying to tell her something.

She thought back to what the sergeant said about forgiving.

She hadn't let go of the anger. *Had she even tried to?* She closed her eyes, remembering her last encounters with Jamie.

Each time Jamie had reached out, Patti slammed the door shut.

Her breath caught as she choked back a sob.

Instead of forgiving, she'd made being hurt and angry a part of her life, a part of her identity. She'd been so self-righteous she'd shut the door on her relationship with Jamie. The few times Jamie had called, she'd been cold and uncommunicative.

Her sister stopped calling.

Jamie hadn't betrayed her, Steven had. For the first time, Patti admitted the truth of it. Patti bowed her head to pray, but the words wouldn't come, only tears. The tears melted the anger and bitterness in her heart. All that remained was worry, sadness, and regret.

Finally, emotions spent, she double-checked the front door's lock and then made her way through the family room. As she walked to the sliding door, she was startled to see a man sitting in a chair.

Her heart raced and she squinted to get a better look.

Sgt. Caldwell was leaning back, watching the night sky.

Another example of her quick rush to judgment.

He was on the patio instead of in his own comfortable bed.

She wondered if she should go out, but decided if he'd wanted her to know he would have told her. Instead, she walked upstairs feeling safe and secure, knowing he was there watching out for them.

She turned towards the guestroom, but stopped at Jamie's bedroom door.

She wasn't ready to go to bed. She should check the room for a clue she might have overlooked. After poking around, it occurred to her that something could be dropped. Patti flopped down and looked under Jamie's bed. A spiral notebook was on the floor under the bed skirt.

Jamie's poetry. She'd been writing poetry since they were children.

Patti had never understood the need. She pulled it out. Noticing a Bible sitting on her sister's nightstand, she picked it up and headed back to her own room.

Patti lay back on the bed and opened the notebook. Just as she'd suspected, it was Jamie's poetry journal. As Patti read through the pages there was a sadness in the words that made her heart ache. But as she continued, the tone of the poetry changed.

In 'The Master Gardener' the words were hopeful.

I want a garden of peace and joy
where it matters not
if the sun shines,
if the rain falls,
if the wind blows.
My life is a rocky patch of dirt and soil
filled with pebbles of pain and problems,
filled with weeds of worry and grief,
filled with rocks of rebellion and wrongdoing.
Nothing good can grow in this rocky patch of mine.
But God is the Master Gardener.
He can change this rocky patch to a garden of peace and joy.

Let God till the dirt and soil.
He can change the weeds of worry to wisdom.
He can change the pebbles of pain to compassion.
He can change the rocks of rebellion to a spirit of submission.

God is the Master Gardener.
He can change that rocky patch to a garden of peace and joy.

Let the Holy Spirit sow the seeds.
He can plant the seeds of forgiveness, mercy, and grace.
He can plant the seeds of goodness, kindness, and faithfulness.
He can plant the seeds of patience, tolerance, and self-control.
God is the Master Gardener.
He can change that rocky patch to a garden of peace and joy.

Let Jesus share the fruits of His labor.
He will give you guidance.
He will give you love and fellowship.
He will give you a friend who never leaves.
God is the Master Gardener.
He can change that rocky patch to a garden of peace and joy.
I found a garden of peace and joy
where it matters not
if the sun shines, the rain falls
or the wind blows.

God is the Master Gardener.

After reading a few more, it was obvious her twin's life had changed. Jamie had developed a personal relationship with Jesus.

Knowing that gave Patti a sense of peace she hadn't felt all day. Her prayers drifted off, sleepily she asked for God's protection for Jamie, Sabrina and…Sgt. Caldwell…

She fell asleep clinging to her sister's Bible.

10

She still clung to the Bible when she woke up the next morning. *Please, God. Let Jamie be home.* She ran to Jamie's bedroom.

The room was empty. *Jamie, Jamie, where are you?*

Finally, she walked in and made Jamie's bed.

Patti fought back tears.

Yesterday, she'd been so angry at Jamie she hadn't wanted to come to Florida. Today, she couldn't think of Jamie without falling apart.

In the kitchen, Anna was at the sink, stacking rinsed dishes in the dishwasher.

Patti looked out the window. Sgt. Caldwell was gone. An unfamiliar warmth tingled in her heart. It had been a long time since she'd had a protector.

"We've already eaten, but you go ahead and eat now," Anna insisted.

Anna placed a chorizo omelet and a bowl of salsa in front of Patti.

It wasn't her usual breakfast fare, but she spooned some on the eggs and discovered it was delicious. "This is great, Anna."

Anna beamed.

Sabrina charged into the kitchen. She wore yellow pajamas with large orange polka dots. Around her neck was a bright red feather boa, and she was wearing a Cleveland Indians baseball cap, which was too big for her head.

"Aunt Patti, you wanna play with me?"

"Not now, *poquita*. Tia Patti is eating."

Sabrina's expression turned into an endearing pout.

"I will as soon as I'm done eating, but only for a little bit, OK? I have some things I need to do."

"Tank you, Aunt Patti."

"Stick your tongue out as you say thank you."

Sabrina gave Patti a stern look and shook her head. "Mommy said sticking out my tongue is bad."

Patti turned her head so Sabrina couldn't see the smile.

She heard Anna chuckling as she washed up dishes at the sink.

"That's not what I...oh, never mind. Your mommy's right. Sorry, I made a mistake."

"Dat's OK, Aunt Patti. You wanna play, now?"

Laughing Anna, told them, "Go ahead, Miss Patti. I'll clean up."

"Anna, you can call me Patti. And thanks for breakfast. It was terrific."

"*De nada.*"

Patti took Sabrina's hand and they walked into the family room. "What do you want to play?"

"Wanna see my doll house?"

"I sure do."

As Patti played with Sabrina, her mind strayed back to Jamie. Surely, there was a clue somewhere. Nobody lived in a complete vacuum. If she worked, she had to have records. If she owned her own business, she still had to have records.

Unless the business was illegal, of course.

But Patti refused to believe such a thing.

Jamie wouldn't be involved in drugs. Her sister

might be flaky and a bit irresponsible, but she never intentionally hurt people.

When Sabrina wandered off to find a new toy, Patti went to find Anna. "I'm going upstairs to look around. If we knew where she worked, we could call them. Maybe they know where she is."

"I wish I could help," Anna said.

Patti walked into Jamie's room. She'd checked the desk and computer the day before, but she hadn't checked everything in the closet.

As soon as she'd found Jamie's purse, she'd called the police and stopped looking.

Moving things around, she looked in shoeboxes but found nothing.

When there was no place left to search in the closet or room, she headed to the adjoining bathroom. The bathroom was amazing. It was almost as large as Patti's bedroom in her house.

Along with a separate shower, Jamie's bathroom had a huge sunken garden tub surrounded by plants and candles. A built-in CD player with a radio and expensive speakers was nestled in the wall by the tub. Of course, only the best for Jamie.

Patti berated herself for her petty jealousy.

She hit the play button. Soothing classical music floated out from the ceiling.

Patti searched the bathroom but saw nothing helpful. As she turned to leave, something caught her eye.

She walked to the tub and inspected the tile. It blended in with the tiles, but there was a door below the tub. Made sense. A plumber needed access to the pipes.

Patti wasn't sure how to open the door. She

pressed all four sides, but that didn't work.

Maybe Anna would know.

She reached to turn off the CD player. One button was unmarked. Patti hit it. The door to the hidden cupboard slid open.

Bending down, she peered into the open compartment.

Inside was a small black suitcase with wheels and a handle. Patti pulled the luggage out and laid it on floor. She unzipped and opened the flap.

After a moment, she let out a low whistle.

Time to call Sgt. Caldwell.

తోల్

Patti paced outside the house. She would let Sgt. Caldwell decide how to proceed.

He pulled up in an older, black, British SUV.

"I found something. It's so bizarre."

"Yeah?" His tone was neutral, but his expression was interrogating.

"Better if you just see it for yourself." She led him in the house.

Anna peeked out of the playroom.

"Better go say hi."

The two of them walked in.

Sabrina leapt to her feet and ran to Sgt. Caldwell as if they'd been friends forever, instead of meeting the previous day. He picked her up and twirled her around.

Sabrina giggled. He squatted down and said, "Hey, Sabrina. Do you remember my name?"

"Your name is powiceman."

"That's my job, not my name. My name is Carter.

Mr. Carter. Can you say that?"

"Mister Tarter," she said proudly.

Carter laughed.

Patti walked over. "Try again, Sabrina. Put your tongue back and say K-k-k-carter."

"K-k-k-tarter." She smiled broadly at the three of them.

"Great, Sabrina. You call me Mr. Tarter and I will call you Sabrina Ballerina."

Sabrina giggled.

"Otay, Mr. Tarter." She ran off to play.

"See you later, Sabrina Ballerina."

She rewarded him with her version of a ballet movement, a twirl and a plie, and then waved before grabbing a doll baby.

"Did you hear something about Miss Jamie?" Anna asked in a hopeful tone as soon as Sabrina was out of earshot.

"No, I just needed Carter...er...Sgt. Caldwell's advice on something I found."

"Carter's my name. Sergeant's my job."

"Anna..." Patti hesitated, looking back and forth between the two, uncertain. "I found something in Jamie's room I need to show *Carter*. You might want to come up, too, if Sabrina can play for a moment without you."

Anna's brow furrowed. "It's her naptime, anyway. I will put her to bed, and then come to Miss Jamie's room."

"You had time the look around more, I take it." Carter said as they walked up the stairs. "Good. The more we find, the more likely we'll be able to figure out this situation. I am beginning to think something is odd about this whole issue."

Patti felt a tug at her heart.

He was confirming her own misgivings, which could mean he'd investigate and together, they'd find her sister.

Together.

Patti turned that over in her mind, wondering if Carter would appreciate how safe he made her feel. She wondered if she should tell him she knew where he'd spent last night. If she said it out loud, it might not feel as special.

She sternly told herself not to get involved with this handsome and charming man. And yet she'd connected with him so quickly, it scared her.

The man was just doing his job. She brushed that thought away, not wanting to deal with it.

She opened Jamie's door and pointed at the suitcase on the bed. "It's over there."

He looked down at the pile of IDs. He picked up a driver's license with Jamie's picture, but with a different name. "Mmm. Interesting. Ms. Jakowski, do you have—"

"If I'm going to call you Carter, then you should call me Patti."

Carter's green eyes twinkled. "Sounds like a deal, Patti. Do you have any idea how she got these?"

She shook her head.

He shuffled through more passports and licenses. "This puts a different light on things, doesn't it?"

Anna came in and stared open-mouthed at the various documents. "*No comprehende.* What does this mean? I have never seen any of this before." She made the sign of the cross.

"OK, Anna." Carter spoke. "When Jamie travels, does she take this suitcase with her?"

"No. She told me she has a small apartment and keeps clothes there. She never take anything with her. Just her purse." Anna looked at him with confusion. "I don't understand this."

"You need to make a list for me of Jamie's friends. Maybe one of them knows something. Speaking of friends, has anybody been calling here looking for Jamie?"

Anna shook her head. "Oh, wait. Mr. Marcus call sometimes to see if Miss Jamie was back, or I heard from her."

"Is that a first or a last name?"

"His name is Marcus Hanks. He and Miss Jamie good friends."

"What kind of friends?" Patti asked.

Could he be the rich boyfriend who'd provided all this luxury for Jamie?

Anna shook her head. "No, no. Not like that. Miss Jamie is friends with whole family."

"That's interesting." Carter said, his expression turning thoughtful. "Can you watch Sabrina for awhile?"

Anna nodded. "Of course, it is my job."

Patti looked at Carter, wondering if he knew this Marcus Hanks. The name had certainly piqued his curiosity.

"Where are you going?" She asked.

"On a fact-finding mission." He had turned into Sgt. Caldwell again, slightly aloof, his mind obviously working out some problem.

"I'm going with you."

"Yes, you most certainly are."

Patti rubbed her arms, goosebumps and all.

What was Jamie doing now? Fake ID's, second

apartments, secret travel plans? Her sister had to be involved in a real mess this time. And now, the cops knew.

The money isn't worth it, Sis.

11

"Where are we going?" Patti asked.

"To unravel another clue." After hitting some keys on the portable computer in his car, Carter mumbled something Patti couldn't hear.

He pulled into a neighborhood more modest than Dolphin Cove. The brick house was beautiful, but not a mansion, like Jamie's.

"I want you to ring the bell and wait for someone to answer. Ask for Marcus Hanks. I'm going to stand behind you just out of sight. If he sees me first, it will ruin the element of surprise."

"Why do we need an element of surprise?" She asked, a little nervous.

"Trust me, we do." He hid to one side.

The door opened. An African-American man, tall, with broad shoulders and a gold loop earring, stood in the doorway. He stared at her for a few seconds.

"What are you doing here, Jamie?" The man snarled through clenched teeth. "I've been looking for you for the past three days. Where have you been?"

"Are you Marcus?" Patti asked.

"Stop playing games, Jamie. You know who I..."

Carter stepped forward and Marcus's voice trailed off.

"Hey, Marcus, let me introduce you to a friend of mine. This is Patti."

"Patti?" The man inspected her. Understanding

dawned in his eyes. "My mistake. I thought you were someone else."

Someone else? How did this man know Jamie? And how did Carter know this man?

"Caldwell, is there a reason you stopped by unannounced? And how did you find out where I lived, anyway? I don't remember ever inviting you here."

"Are you done with your questions, Marcus? Because I have a few of my own."

"This is a bad time, Carter. I'll call you tomorrow when it's a work day." Marcus moved to close the door.

Carter put out a hand to stop the door from closing. "Not tomorrow, Marcus. Now."

"Let's talk outside." He turned. "Honey, I've got some business to take care of."

"Is everything OK, Marcus?" A woman's voice floated out.

"Yes, it's fine. I'm going to be outside talking a little business with an old friend."

Patti sneaked a glance at Carter.

He didn't look worried.

Marcus led them to some benches on one side of the house.

Patti sat down, very aware of Carter's thigh touching hers when he sat, too.

Marcus tapped his foot against another bench. Built like a football lineman, with his bald head and shiny gold earring, he looked intimidating.

"OK, Marcus. Tell me what's going on."

"I don't know what you mean. You're the one who brought your date to my house. Uninvited, I might add."

"Let's start with why you called Patti, Jamie?" Carter's voice took on an edge. "How do you know Jamie?"

"I'm the one asking the questions."

"Patti is Jamie's sister," Carter told Marcus.

"Yep. I see that."

"Well, you FBI types are a little slow, sometimes."

FBI?

Patti stared.

What did Jamie have to do with the FBI?

"Patti flew from Ohio to file a missing person report on her sister."

Blood drained from Marcus's face. "Are you sure?"

"We're sure. What's going on?"

"What makes you think she's missing?"

Carter glanced at Patti, then explained Sabrina's phone call, Anna's misgivings, Patti's arrival, and the suitcase full of IDs.

"With all the security in that development, how could this happen? We picked the place because of its elaborate security system."

"I might have a theory, Marcus," Carter said. "The beach."

"The beach? It's locked and gated even on the beach side."

"Last night we…took a walk…and found the gate wide open. Anyone could have walked in. The security camera was probably broken the night she disappeared. And there's a marina not even half a mile from the beach entrance. They could have taken her to a waiting boat in a matter of minutes."

"It's possible, but they would still need to get her to the beach without being seen."

"It wouldn't have been all that difficult depending on the time. A lot of the residents drive golf carts. There'd been a report about a repairman in the area, but that checked out to be legit."

"I suppose it's possible. I need to make some calls, and then we can talk. I'll be back in a few." Marcus strode off towards his front door.

"We'll be waiting," Carter said.

"So, you do think Jamie was abducted," Patti said.

"I didn't want to alarm you, but the purse thing bothered me, too. I did a little investigating."

"Thank you, Carter. I don't know…"

He tipped an imaginary cowboy hat and tried to do a John Wayne imitation. "Just doing my job, Ma'am."

"Who is Marcus?" Patti asked quickly, touched by his attempt to put her at ease, but still wary of this too handsome man.

"He's an FBI agent and the liaison with our police department. When Anna said he was a friend of Jamie's, I knew more was going on than a runaway mom."

"Why would an FBI agent know Jamie?" Patti knew nothing about Jamie anymore.

Somewhere along the way, they'd become two strangers who shared the same DNA.

Guilt knocked at her heart's door.

"Do you think Jamie works for the FBI, or what?"

"It's a possibility. Or Marcus might be investigating Jamie…"

Investigating Jamie?

"You're probably right."

The door opened again, and Marcus walk down the steps towards them, his mouth set in a grim line.

"What's going on?" Carter asked.

Patti waited to hear the words to make everything all right.

Jamie was fine and would be home soon.

There'd just been a mix-up and it was all a silly mistake—a canceled flight, a sudden illness, a last minute delay.

She willed him to say the words.

"Let's take a walk around back." Marcus motioned with his head.

Patti's hope flickered out.

He led them to a garden lush with roses, begonias, ferns and other exotic plants. He motioned to a cast iron bistro set nestled in the garden.

Once they were situated, Marcus's fingers drummed on the table top. "Let me assure you we already have people searching for Jamie. When she didn't check in with me yesterday as scheduled, I assumed she was just busy. It happens, sometimes. We'll do everything we can to find her."

Patti's heart sank.

Jamie was in serious trouble.

Patti couldn't deny the truth any longer.

"I don't understand. Does she work for you or what?"

Marcus's gold earring glittered in the bright Florida sun. "Not exactly," he said, but the hesitation in his voice told her there was more.

"What does 'not exactly' mean, Marcus?"Carter asked. "How do you not exactly work for the FBI?"

Marcus ran his fingers along the black laced ironwork of the table. "She's an informant." Marcus finally answered. "A really good informant. You won't find her name on any official FBI employee list but, yes, she definitely works for us."

"An informant?"

"I can't go into all the details, but I'll tell you what I can. Several years ago, I met Jamie during the course of an investigation. When I confronted her about the illegal activities of her then-current boyfriend, she was so disturbed, I believed her when she said she didn't know anything.

"Instead of arresting her, I asked if she'd help and she did. Within a few weeks, Jamie provided us with the proof we needed to arrest and convict the man."

He paused and stared hard at Patti and Carter. "This next part is privileged information. If you tell anyone, I'll deny it. Understand?"

They both nodded.

"Because she was so helpful, I forgot to name her as a party to the investigation, and so the government didn't confiscate the property, or money her friend gave her as gifts."

No one said anything for a few moments.

Patti turned towards Carter and found him staring at her.

He had come to the same conclusion.

"Is that how she got the money for her house, for the way she lives?" Patti demanded, her voice getting louder with each word. "Being a paid—"

Marcus cut her off. His eyes flashed with anger. "She is no such thing. She's a patriot helping her country, but, yes that is partly how she got some of her money"

"Partly? What do you mean partly?"

"Your sister is a whiz at investing. It's become quite the lucrative hobby for her." He pointed at his house, which Patti now realized was more than most government workers could afford. "And for me. She took the paltry sum I gave her and turned it into some very serious money," Marcus told Patti. "She also knew when to liquidate her funds."

"Are you trying to tell me she got rich from investing, and not from...from..." Patti searched for the right words. "Not from doing favors for the FBI?"

"It was mostly from investing, but she helped us out a few more times over the years." He paused, frowning. "It's unorthodox, but she's a born actress."

So, Jamie had fulfilled her dream to be an actress, just not the way she'd planned. And she'd become wealthy in the process.

"Jamie's helped us put away some nasty people."

Time slowed as the meaning of his words hit her. Aware of the fragrance of the roses, of the glaring sunlight, of the slight breeze blowing her hair, she played the words over in her mind.

Her sister was in more danger than Patti ever imagined.

"Any of them could have wanted revenge. Any of them could have kidnapped her or...or...worse."

Carter reached out and touched Patti's arm.

She gave him a grateful look.

Marcus stood and paced around the garden, picking off a dead flower here and there. "They had no idea Jamie was involved with us."

"One of them found out." Carter said in a quiet tone. "It would explain her disappearance."

"There's a small possibility, but other than the original incident, we provided her with new identities." He plucked off a dead flower from the hydrangea, and then walked back to his chair.

"We found the stash of ID's at her house," Patti

said.

Marcus's gaze met Patti's.

More bad news.

Marcus ran his hand over his bald head. "She never used her own identity except for the first time, and the case she's working on, this time."

"What's she working on?" Carter asked.

"I'm not at liberty to discuss that," Marcus said.

"Not at liberty," Patti jumped up and yelled.

Both men wore shocked expressions as her chair fell over.

"My sister is missing, and you aren't at liberty to discuss it with me? I don't think so. This...this...isn't right. I have a right to know. You can't just say you're hunting for her and expect me to not ask any questions."

"I'm sorry, but it has to be this way. I'll keep you informed, but I can't give you any details."

"Not good enough," Carter said.

"It has to be, Carter. I can't tell you anymore. We are doing all that can be done."

"That's it. I'm supposed to sit here while you claim you're looking for my sister." She moved back to the table, but didn't sit down.

"I'm not claiming anything," Frustration edged his voice. "We are looking for your sister. Jamie and I are friends, close friends, in fact. She and Sabrina are a part of my family."

"Really. That's why you set her up with drug lords and who-knows-what other criminals because you are such close friends."

"Your sister is a courageous woman who believes in doing the right thing. And, in fact, I tried to get her to give up this job, but she refused because she understood the importance of what she was doing." Marcus said, and then paused. "Where's Sabrina now?"

"She's at the house with Anna."

"I don't think it's a good idea for Sabrina and Anna to stay there. It might not be safe."

12

Patti heard the words "might not be safe." Her mind couldn't grasp the enormity of their meaning. As the words soaked into her consciousness, her legs wouldn't hold her up any longer and she sank back down in the chair. Her stomach churned. "You mean Sabrina and Anna could be in danger at this moment?"

"It's possible. We have to assume Jamie didn't leave of her own free will."

Panic threatened to overwhelm her. Breathing went shallow and rapid. "I can't believe this." Her head was spinning.

"Patti, put your head down. Take a deep breath." Carter rubbed her back.

Thoughts swirled around, threatening to drown her. *Stop it. You aren't the important one at the moment. Sabrina and Anna aren't safe. Have to go help them.* Keeping her eyes closed, she ran through the words of her favorite praise song. Her breathing slowed and she opened her eyes.

"Thanks, Carter. I'm OK. We have to go get them. Right now."

"Carter and I will go." Marcus stood. "You better stay here with my wife."

"I'm going with you."

"I don't have time to argue. I'll be right behind you. I have a couple of other calls to make. "

In seconds, Patti and Carter were in his car.

Carter reached under her seat, pulled out a siren, and then plopped it on top of the car.

"This isn't a game. You do exactly what I tell you to do. Understand?"

"I get it."

"You stay in the car. I'll let you know when it's safe."

"No way, she's my niec—"

"That's my job, Patti."

She hadn't been there for Jamie. She would make sure she was there for Jamie's daughter.

"I'm going with you."

"You stay behind me at all times. Got it?"

He slowed as he approached an intersection, but swerved around other cars, fishtailed, and kept going.

She clutched the door handle.

Carter tossed her a cell phone. "Call Dolphin Cove and tell them to put up their gate because we're not stopping. Hit send, the number's right there."

"Shouldn't I tell them to go to Jamie's house? They could—"

"They're rent-a-cops. They could make the situation worse."

As she called the palm trees come into view. *Hurry. Hurry. Please keep them safe, God.*

The car slowed slightly as they rounded the corner and fishtailed once more.

Carter reached up and shut off the siren. "We don't want to alert them."

"Makes sense." She prayed this man was as capable as he seemed to be.

As they sped down the palm-lined drive, the gate moved up and then they were through.

Moments later, the car skidded to a stop in front of

Jamie's home.

Carter was out of the car and moving towards the house before she'd unbuckled her seat belt.

"Stay back," he whispered, then sprinted toward the door.

She caught up.

He pulled out his gun. He opened the door inch by inch. He looked back and put a finger to his mouth.

Her heart pounded. *Please let them be OK.*

He moved through the door with the stealth of a lion circling its prey.

She followed.

No one in the living room. No one in the kitchen. Down the hall to the family room. An open door.

Patti gasped as she entered the room.

Anna lay on the floor bleeding and moaning.

Sabrina wasn't in the room.

A soft breeze made her look towards the sliding door. It was open.

Carter stopped and leaned over Anna, feeling her pulse. "Call 911 and get something to stop the bleeding." He patted Anna, but her eyes were glazed over. "Anna, Anna. Where's Sabrina?"

No response.

Patti stood rooted to the spot.

Some monster had Sabrina.

Her mind was blank, unable to process the horror.

Carter stood and gave her a gentle push. "Get towels. Stop the bleeding. Remember your first aid classes. Apply pressure to the wound. I'm going outside to look for Sabrina."

Patti blinked. She nodded at Carter, to let him know she heard him. Speech was impossible right now.

Sabrina's baby doll blanket lay on the floor.

She grabbed it and dashed back to Anna, knelt and put pressure against the wound. Wordless images flowed through her brain, silent snapshots of her little niece, her sister, imagined terror, heart-pounding fear. Tears leaked.

Carter was gone.

She grabbed her cell phone and dialed 911. She heard a noise from behind.

Must be Marcus .He said he'd be right—The phone slipped from her hand. It wasn't Marcus.

The jogger from the beach stood there, holding Sabrina with a hand clasped around her mouth and a knife to her throat.

Patti gasped as all the breath left her body.

Sabrina's little body shook with sobs, tears flowing over the man's hand.

Her pressure on Anna's wound slipped. As she stood and faced him, he kicked out, connecting with her ribs.

Patti gasped in pain, nearly doubling over.

"Get up. I don't have time for any nonsense. I'm just going to tell you once. If you do anything I don't like, I will kill her. You want that to happen?"

"No." Patti gasped out, clutching her side.

"Let's go. Go to the kitchen and into the garage."

Her shoes felt as if they were filled with wet sand. Looking around, her gaze landed on the carving knives on the counter. Maybe, she could grab one, but what then?

He had a knife to Sabrina's throat.

She couldn't take a chance.

One step at a time, she moved towards the garage door. There was no way she could save Sabrina from this madman. Hopeless despair washed through her body. Patti stumbled.

He shoved her. "Faster. When you get in the garage, get in the car. You're going to drive us. Got it? Grab the keys."

She took the keys off the hook by the garage door. Opening the door, she stepped through. Her peripheral vision caught a movement to her side.

Thank you, God.

Carter pointed in the opposite direction.

She turned towards the left and moved fast to draw the jogger's attention away from Carter.

"Not that way, you stupid—." The man yelled as he turned towards her, but in the next moment Carter's gun was against the man's back.

"Police. Drop the knife and let go of the child."

The man dropped Sabrina and bolted.

Sabrina ran to Carter.

Carter peeled her little arms away, and then passed her off to Patti.

"Take care of Anna and Sabrina." Carter ordered and ran after the man.

Patti squeezed the little girl to her. "It's OK, sweetie. You're safe now. The bad man's gone."

"He hurt Anna." Sabrina cried. "Anna."

"It's OK, sweetie. Let's go help—"

Police cars and emergency vehicles pulled into the drive.

Marcus Hanks dashed into the garage. He pointed his gun towards the ceiling. "Where's Carter?"

"Chasing him," she said, startled at her now calm tone. "Anna's hurt."

"EMTs are here." He waved towards the ambulance. "Which way did they go?"

"I don't know."

Marcus turned and ran in Carter's general direction.

Patti hugged Sabrina to her.

Thank you, God, for keeping her safe.

She was brought back to reality by Sabrina's tiny voice.

"I can't bweathe, Aunt Patti. You're squeezing me too hard."

~⚮~

Carter couldn't believe the man, whom he recognized as the jogger from the night before, had disappeared. He'd known there was something wrong about him. And there must have been an accomplice waiting in a vehicle in case he needed to flee.

Police officers of all types had descended on Dolphin Cove.

Marcus stood in Jamie's yard giving directions to one man, and then another.

Carter walked up to him. "Sorry, Marcus. He got away."

"How'd that happen?"

"I think he had an accomplice waiting."

"I'll have someone check the security video. We might get a break and find ID of the car they left in." Marcus turned back to a uniformed officer, answered his question, and then turned back to Carter. "Don't worry about it, man. You did the important part. You kept Sabrina and Patti safe."

"Anna?"

"On her way to the hospital. Knife wound. The EMTs said she should be OK." Marcus pointed towards the house. "Sabrina and Patti are inside."

Carter went through the door.

Sabrina sat in Patti's lap sobbing.

He folded both of them in his arms.

Patti kept her voice low. "I didn't know what to do when I saw you standing there."

"You were perfect. It was exactly what I wanted you to do. The whole thing shouldn't have happened."

"What are you talking about? You saved us. If you weren't here, he'd have taken both of us. You're a hero."

"Some hero. I shouldn't have left you alone in the first place."

Sabrina looked up and lurched toward Carter. Carter wrapped her in his arms and squeezed her tight.

Patti and Carter's eyes met over Sabrina's head.

Patti reached up and touched his cheek. "Not true. You thought he'd left with Sabrina. You had to follow him."

"I should have—"

"Stop it, Carter. You did the right thing. You aren't in control of everything." Marcus Hanks stood beside them. "Got it?"

"Yeah, I got it." He stood, holding Sabrina, who now clasped his neck.

"We need to get to the hospital to check on Anna," Patti said.

"Not without an escort." Marcus told her. "Let's go. I'll drive."

Holding Sabrina in one arm, Carter put his other arm around Patti as they walked out.

She moved in closer to him.

13

Patti sat in the hospital waiting room holding Sabrina.

The knife missed all of Anna's vital organs and the surgeon expected a full recovery.

As Patti rocked Sabrina and hummed softly in her ear, Marcus and Carter sat in a corner of the room whispering.

Sabrina clung to Patti, her eyes haunted. "I want Mommy." She whispered once before the events of the day overtook her. She relaxed against Patti's body in an exhausted sleep.

Patti lay Sabrina on a small couch before she went over to the men. "What's happening?"

"That's what we're discussing. We're going to put a guard with Anna, and we're going to place you and Sabrina in a safe house." Marcus told her.

"A safe house?"

"It's a place—"

"I know what it is. I watch TV."

"Jamie worked hard to keep her private life and her work life totally separate from each other. But it seems her two worlds have collided in a big way." His eyes met Patti's. "She understood it wouldn't be safe for others so she made the decision to stay away from friends and...and family."

The meaning of those words sank in.

Patti wiped away the tears. Her next words were

barely audible. "Is that why she stayed away from me?"

Marcus nodded slowly. "She couldn't bear to part with Sabrina, but knew it was safer if she stayed away from you for the time being. Her plan was to finish her current project and then leave the job permanently."

"Was her plan?" Patti asked.

"I'm sure it still is her plan. I didn't mean..." Marcus wouldn't meet Patti's gaze. His voice became all business. "Anyway, we need to make plans for the three of you."

No one spoke.

Patti broke the silence. "I want to know what's going on. What was she doing that was...is so important?"

Marcus didn't answer.

Patti's heart was breaking but she forced herself to say the words. She matched stares with Marcus. "You think she's dead, don't you?"

Marcus looked up at the ceiling. Long moments passed before he turned back to Patti. "I'm not going to lie to you. It's a possibility, but at this point it's hard to say. I haven't given up hope and neither should you."

Carter laid a hand on her back, and his touch calmed her.

"If she worked so hard at keeping her identity secret, why is she using her own name this time?" Carter asked.

"That's a good question," Patti looked back at Marcus. "And if she was so worried about me, why wasn't she as worried about Sabrina?"

"She was, but Sabrina was her daughter. She couldn't abandon her. We took every precaution we could to keep Sabrina and Anna safe. The house has an elaborate security system. She lived in a gated community. Her work was...was in another state. When she traveled, she traveled under other names and always took several flights using different names, before getting to her final destination."

"But it wasn't enough to keep her safe."

"No, it wasn't."

"You didn't answer the other part of the question." Carter pointed out. "Why was she working under her own name this time?"

Marcus looked at Carter, then at Patti. "I can't give you the details, but Jamie knew the man socially before he came under investigation so he already knew her real name. She happened to run into him, and she overheard something which made her suspicious."

"What's the story on him?" Carter asked.

"I didn't want Jamie to get involved with him again," Marcus murmured more to himself than to Carter and Patti. "I had a bad feeling. I told her to go home and forget about him, but she refused to listen to me." He focused back on Patti. "Don't get me wrong. I'm not making excuses. I take full responsibility for...for the investigation."

Her sister—an FBI informant—living a double life. The thought boggled her mind.

Carter interrupted her thoughts. "Marcus, you didn't answer my question. Who's this man, and why are you investigating him?"

"Can't tell you." Marcus's tone was adamant.

"You have to tell us. How are we going to find Jamie, if you don't?" Patti said through clenched teeth.

"The whole FBI is looking for her," Marcus pointed out. "I'll handle the investigation. In the meantime, I'll arrange for you, Sabrina, and Anna, as soon as she is released, to go to a safe house."

"You should do what Marcus says," Carter agreed. "We can keep all of you safe. No more nasty surprises."

"You need to arrange a place for Sabrina and Anna." Patti shook her head. "But I'm not going into hiding. I'm helping with the investigation."

"Absolutely not," Marcus and Carter said in unison.

They all looked towards Sabrina but she was still asleep.

"Yes, I am," she whispered. "My sister is missing, and I'm not leaving until we find her."

"Not a good idea, Patti," Carter said.

"Why not?" she demanded, furious the two men were forming a united front.

"It's not safe," Marcus told her.

"I won't stay at the house. I'll go find a hotel somewhere, but I'm not leaving." She folded her arms across her chest to emphasize the point.

"Patti, Jamie is your identical twin," Carter told her in a soft voice. "You can't be running around here. It could cause problems for you."

Patti's eyes filled with tears. "But Jamie needs me."

"You're right, Jamie does need you." Carter touched her arm. "She needs you to take care of Sabrina and Anna right now, and she wouldn't want you to put yourself in danger. After all, she worked very hard to keep you out of this mess. You owe it to her to take care of Sabrina."

She met Carter's gaze. "Fine, I'll go with them."

Fifteen minutes later, the nurse came to tell them Anna was in her room and they could visit.

When Patti walked in, Anna looked tired and pale. "Sabrina?" But she didn't need to answer because Patti showed her Sabrina, now sleeping on her shoulder.

Anna gave a weak grin. "She is safe."

"Carter stopped the man from taking Sabrina."

"What did the man want? Why..."

"I can't tell you, Anna." Holding her hand, Marcus flashed his badge.

"FBI." Anna's gaze turned panicked. "I thought you were a businessman."

"I know. I'm sorry we deceived you, but Jamie didn't want you to know how dangerous her job was. She didn't want you worried and upset every time she left, because Sabrina might pick up on it. Her goal was to let Sabrina have as normal a life as possible."

Anna bit her lip

"Are you in pain, Anna? Should I call the nurse?" Patti asked.

"No, just tired."

"Well, you get your rest. Sabrina and Patti are staying with you. There's an armed guard outside. No one's going to hurt any of you again," Carter assured her.

Anna's eyes fluttered and a moment later, her breathing relaxed.

Carter turned toward Marcus. "Can you take me back to my car?"

"Sure thing. I'll go get the car and pick you up by the emergency room."

After Marcus left, Carter took Patti's hand in his own and led her away from Anna's bed. "Are you all right?"

She refused to cry. "I can't tell you how grateful I am for you helping us. I can't imagine what might have happened if you hadn't been there."

He moved closer and put his arms on her shoulders. "Don't think all the things that could have happened. Stay focused on the fact you're all safe. I'm glad I've been there for all of you."

All of us, except Jamie.

His arms moved around her. She leaned against him, gaining strength.

After a moment, he broke the connection. "You're safe here. There are two guards outside the door. If you need anything, one will get it while the other stays with you. I hate to leave you, but..."

"It's OK, Carter. We're safe and we're together."

"Is there anything I can get you before I come back?"

"Maybe some of Sabrina's toys, if you want."

He grinned and her heart melted.

He might be one of the bravest men she'd ever known.

14

Sabrina sat with arms folded across her chest. "Me don't want to go. I want Mommy."

Patti smiled. This little girl knew a thing or two about getting her own way.

"Now, pumpkin face, you know Mommy has to go on trips for work," Marcus said patiently.

"She didn't say goodbye." Her lower lip poked out in a pout.

Patti had become very familiar with that pout over the past few days.

Sabrina knew how to manipulate others. But it was so adorable, it was hard to resist.

"That's because she told me to tell you goodbye," Marcus told her.

Sabrina buried her face in Marcus's neck and sobbed.

Patti's heart broke for the little girl. She really wanted her sister back home with her and Sabrina.

Anna was being discharged that day, and it was time to move to a safe house.

Thanks to the posted guards, there'd been no incidents at the hospital.

Sabrina lifted her head and looked at Marcus. "Where's Mister Tarter? Me want Mister Tarter. He saved me from the mean man." Over the past two days, Sabrina had developed a case of hero worship.

Patti couldn't really blame her niece.

During their confinement in the hospital, he'd brought them food, toys, books, and magazines.

Patti couldn't have survived without his visits or his smile.

"Yes, he did, pumpkin face, and he'll be here any minute. He wanted to say goodbye before you go on your trip."

A few minutes later, the door opened.

When Carter walked in Sabrina launched herself at him. He caught her and twirled her around.

"If it isn't Sabrina Ballerina. You look mighty beautiful today."

She giggled. "You wook mi...mi..mighty beautiful today."

"Me, beautiful. You must have me mistaken for someone else."

Another twirl and she giggled more.

Even Anna laughed, holding her stomach as she did.

"I need to talk with Patti. We'll be out in a minute."

Marcus nodded.

Anna and Sabrina left with Marcus, leaving Patti and Carter alone.

They stood facing each other.

"I know this isn't what you expected."

"Jamie's my sister." Patti cut him off. "And stop apologizing. If it hadn't been for you..." Her mind flashed to the man holding a knife to Sabrina. "If it hadn't been for you, Sabrina could have been hurt. You kept her safe."

"But not Anna."

"Anna's alive. That's all that matters."

He nodded. "Keep praying. Don't forget God's in

control."

"I just…so much has happened. This whole thing is so…unbelievable."

Carter wrapped his arms around her.

After a moment, Patti took a few steps away from him. She smiled, but inside all she felt was sadness. How she wished she'd met him under different circumstances.

"I promise I'm going to do everything I can to find Jamie." He paused. "But I can't promise…"

She understood the unspoken words.

"We won't be able to talk while you're in the safe house. You'll have to rely on the FBI agents to call me if you need something from me."

He was still trying to take care of them.

"I sure had you pegged wrong the first day I met you."

"How exactly did you peg me, if I might ask?"

Her mouth opened but she closed it as she searched for something to say without admitting what she'd thought. "Never mind."

"Mmm. Very interesting. I won't pursue this line of questioning at the moment, ma'am, but we are not done with this conversation."

Giving a hint of a smile, she realized she might find herself admitting more to him than she cared to.

They walked out to the car in a sweet silence.

Carter sat in the front seat while Marcus drove.

Not wanting to alarm Sabrina, Patti sang songs with her in the back seat.

Anna sat beside Patti staring out the window.

Behind them the other agents followed in a second car.

Marcus's cell phone shattered the silence, making

both Patti and Anna jump. The phone call lasted all of ten seconds.

Marcus flipped the phone shut and looked over at Carter. "We've got company."

"What's going on?" Patti asked.

"Someone's following us."

Anna muttered something in Spanish and crossed herself.

"What are we going to do?" Patti's heart raced and she wiped sweaty palms on her jeans. She fought the urge to turn around.

"Let's go to police headquarters."

"What are you guys talking about?"

Carter patted her hand resting on the back of the seat. His calmness lessened her jitters.

"We're going to drive to headquarters and go into the underground parking. It's impossible for them to follow us in there. We're going to switch cars and as we leave several other cars are going to come out with us."

"I don't get it."

"They can't follow all of us. You're going to hide so they have to pick one car to follow. If we're lucky, they won't pick the right one. Once they choose the wrong car, it's free sailing for us and we'll have another car stop them. And if we're lucky, put an end to this nightmare."

"What if they pick the car we are in?"

"We'll cross that bridge when we come to it," Marcus told her.

Once they were in the underground parking lot, Carter ran upstairs.

In five minutes, three more officers appeared with keys in their hands.

They spent another ten minutes debating on which cars to make the decoy cars, which car would be the real getaway vehicle.

In the end, they decided Marcus, Patti, and her group would be in one of the officers' vehicles, an SUV, so Anna could be somewhat comfortable while laying down.

Marcus, Patti, and Sabrina scrunched down in the backseat so they wouldn't be seen.

Carter took a squad car.

Sabrina slept through the vehicle switch.

Thirty minutes later, Patti's leg cramped from being scrunched on the floor. She tapped Marcus on the shoulder and whispered. "I've got to move my leg."

"It's OK. You can get up. They aren't anywhere around. They followed Caldwell." The driver of the truck announced.

Marcus lifted himself off the floor while the women situated themselves.

The ruse worked, but the car had evaded the police and escaped.

They were no closer to figuring out who was after them.

❧

Marcus hurried them out of the truck and towards the entrance.

Patti stared at the old apartment building. *This was it?* A knot in her stomach formed. The placed didn't look all that safe.

Once inside, Marcus herded them to a waiting elevator and hit the fifth floor button.

Anna's gaze met Patti's as if they had the same thought.

How could a simple apartment building like this keep Sabrina safe when Jamie's elaborate security system, with an on-site security force, hadn't?

The elevator bumped to a stop and the door slid open.

Two agents stood in front of the elevator. Each faced the opposite direction as if they were bookends.

Seeing their guns drawn made Patti queasy. She pressed Sabrina's head against her chest, hoping to keep her from noticing the weapons.

They stopped in front of a door with 507 in big black letters on it.

The lead agent opened the door and herded the group in.

Patti set Sabrina down and her stomach unknotted somewhat.

There was a square living room with a simple sofa and matching chair. A coffee table, end tables and a TV against the opposite wall rounded out the ordinary furnishings.

A small dinette sat behind the sofa in front of the sole window. To the right was a kitchen. A hallway led to what Patti guessed were the bedrooms and bathroom.

The whole apartment could fit into Jamie's front room.

"It's not much but..." Marcus walked in behind them. "At least you'll be safe."

"How do you know?" Patti wasn't convinced. "It seems like it would be easy—"

"It's not. Trust me. You'll be fine."

"I felt safer at the hospital than here."

Anna looked at the two of them and grabbed Sabrina's hand, leading her towards the back of the apartment. "Let's go look at the rest of the apartment, *poquita*."

"Patti, you're safe." Marcus' voice was patient.

"The way Jamie was safe at Dolphin Cove?" She stomped off to look out the one window in the apartment. She'd feel safer if Carter was here.

A moment later, Marcus put a hand on her shoulder.

She turned. "Are you going to stay with us?"

"I can't. I'm going to lead the search for Jamie."

"Maybe I'd feel safer if Carter stayed with us? After all, he's proven himself more than once."

"I'll see what I can do, but in the meantime you're out of harm's way. We've got two guards posted outside the apartment at all times." He pointed at the window. "As you can see no one is going to come in from that direction. I've got to get going but I want to say goodbye to Sabrina." Marcus left, then walked back carrying Sabrina.

"I want to stay with you." Sabrina clung to Marcus.

Patti's heart cracked. She'd been through so much. It was obvious she was terrified.

"I love you. I will see you soon." Marcus said, as he set her down. "You be a good little girl for Anna and Aunt Patti."

"I not a little girl. I a big girl," Sabrina said with hands on her tiny hips.

"Of course, Sabrina, that's what I meant. You are a big girl." Marcus chuckled and gave her another hug. Over Sabrina's head, he looked at the two women. "I'll call the minute I know anything."

The moment he was gone, Anna threw up her hands. "I cannot believe this. Mr. Marcus and Miss Jamie working for the FBI. I did not know any of this. Miss Jamie must be in *mucho* danger." Tears trickled from Anna's eyes. "I should have known."

"Jamie was trying to protect you."

"Miss Patti. I have something for you. I hope you will not be mad at me. I am sorry I didn't deliver it to you sooner, but Jamie told me to give it to you if something ever happened to her. I didn't want to do it in front of the policeman, or Mr. Marcus. And then I got hurt and couldn't give it to you." Anna handed over an envelope.

When Patti touched the envelope she shivered as if someone had walked over a grave. Not her grave. Jamie's.

The little energy she had seeped out of her. Sitting down on the sofa, she opened the envelope and found a slip of paper and a key.

Her heart fluttered as she looked at her sister's handwriting.

2057 Southern-Abby Lane #411.

Nothing more on the paper. There wasn't a city or state, but it had to be important.

The key could go to an apartment or house that Jamie lived in when she was out of town. Excitement surged through Patti. If she could discover where Jamie lived, maybe she could find Jamie.

A sense of futility came over Patti. She would never be able to find Jamie on her own. She didn't know the first thing about finding missing people. She was a counselor at a high school, not a private detective.

But Carter would know what to do.

15

The next morning, Patti was up long before Anna or Sabrina. Too many things were on her mind to allow sleep. The address changed everything. Giving it to Marcus wasn't an option.

Carter would help her. He'd promised.

When Sabrina stumbled into the room hand-in-hand with Anna, Patti already had sausage and pancakes cooking.

Sabrina ran over to Patti and gave her a hug. "Good morning, Aunt Patti."

"Hey, sweetie. I hope you're hungry. I cooked breakfast for you," Patti said with forced cheerfulness.

After breakfast, Patti broke the news.

"Sweetie?"

"What?"

"I have to go away for a few days, but Anna is going to stay here."

"You cannot leave. We are..." Anna gave a meaningful look at Sabrina who sat eating a pancake. "We are s-a-f-e. You need to stay here, too. Mr. Marcus said so."

"I have to try and help. I can't just sit here and do nothing." Patti attempted to keep her voice casual.

"This is no good. Mr. Marcus did not think it was a good idea. Better for you to stay here, with us."

Sabrina's eyes were wide as they moved from Anna to Patti and back again.

"It's OK, Sabrina. Anna and I are just talking." Patti took her plate to the sink and rinsed the dish. "I can help. I'm going to call Carter. He'll know what to do with the address and key."

Anna nodded.

"Anna, how does Jamie wear her hair?"

"It is shorter than yours. It comes to her shoulder." Anna gestured with her hands.

"Bangs or no bangs?"

"This is not good, Miss Patti. You need to..." Anna threw up her hands in frustration. "No bangs. She go to Jean-Pierre's."

"Where's that?"

"He's in the phone book. I don't see how you can leave. Those FBI men won't let you leave."

"Yeah, that's a problem, but I've been thinking."

Anna's gaze reminded Patti of her mother's after she and Jamie had done one of their many pranks. "I'm sure you have."

"You invite them in for coffee and breakfast." She pointed at the leftover pancakes and sausage. "If they ask about me, tell them I'm taking a bath. I'll slip out while they're eating, and they won't have to know."

Anna muttered in Spanish and crossed herself.

"We have to do this for Jamie."

Anna nodded her agreement.

Patti got her purse and hid in a closet by the door. For a moment, she lost her nerve.

But Jamie was out there somewhere and needed her.

Tears threatened, but she took a deep breath. It was time to do something to help Jamie. If Jamie could be brave and courageous, so could she.

After all, they shared the same genes.

❧❧

Carter Caldwell glared at the phone.

Marcus Hanks had called. The FBI thought he might compromise the investigation. He was no longer on the case.

He had no plans to break the promise he had given to Patti. It would be easier with the FBI cooperating, but he wasn't without his own resources.

He'd missed talking with her last night. Her quick wit and warmth came through each time they talked. He'd become accustomed to spending time with her and Sabrina. Visiting them at the hospital had been the highlight of each day, but no phone calls were allowed while they were at the safe house.

He turned back to his computer.

The door opened and his boss walked in.

"Hey, Chief, what brings you down to my office?"

"Caldwell, this office should be condemned." Carter's boss shook his head as he looked around the room.

"I know. I know. As soon as I get some time, I'll get it organized."

"Good to hear, because as of now, you've got the time."

"I'm busy with the Jakowski disappearance."

"No, you're not." He made an elaborate show of looking at his watch and then back at Carter. "As of this moment, you are officially off the case. In fact, there is no case. You need to dump that file in the trash and forget you ever heard the name."

Carter's blood boiled.

Marcus had gone over his head.

He should have known better than to trust him.

"No way. I started this case and I'm going to—"

"You are done investigating that case." The tone of the police chief was firm.

They glared at each other.

"That's an order, Carter."

"You're going to turn your back on this?"

"I have no choice in the matter, and neither do you. We both know things like this happen in the real world. Even I have a boss."

"But—"

"No buts, Carter. When Homeland Security calls these days, you do what they ask if you value your job."

"Homeland Security?"

"That's what I said. They wouldn't give details. You are officially assigned to this hog-sty you call an office for the next three days. You get this office cleaned up and stop investigating. Otherwise, you're going to be reassigned to permanent desk duty. Got it?"

"I hear you, Chief."

❧

Patti waited.

The guards had refused offers of breakfast. Now it was time for Plan B.

Anna was in Sabrina's room explaining they were going to play a little game to make sure the policeman were doing their job.

She took a deep breath and waited, peeking through the slats of the closet door.

A blood-curdling yell came from Anna, and then

from Sabrina.

The front door opened and the two guards rushed in.

Quietly, she opened the closet door, then the front door. She ran as fast as she could. Once the stairwell door closed, she took a deep breath and waited for the pounding of her heart to slow down.

16

The bright afternoon Florida sun beat down on Patti as she walked from the beauty salon. Ohio's winters might be brutal, but so was this heat.

She looked back at the salon and gave a little wave to the man staring out at her. It hadn't been easy to get an appointment the same day, but Jean-Pierre agreed only because she was Jamie's sister. And like everyone else, he loved Jamie.

Patti walked towards the car she'd rented.

With her hair cut shorter and layered, Patti's natural curl came to life.

Jean-Pierre put in a few highlights to match Jamie's sun-lightened hair.

Patti had to admit it looked and felt great, but she'd been shocked at the price. She wrote out a check that would cover her own grocery bill for a month. Money couldn't buy happiness, but it sure could buy beauty.

She wondered if Carter would like it.

What a ridiculous thought.

Carter Caldwell might be handsome and charming, but that was as far as it could ever go. His smile and sparkling green eyes popped up in her mind's eye.

She liked the man, more than she cared to admit. But there was no future for the two of them. Patti needed to keep reminding herself lest she forget it.

She had to find Jamie, to act as bait to lure the killer...no, kidnapper, into the open.

But first, she needed to find this address. Hopefully, it would lead her to where Jamie worked.

At the police station, Patti headed back to Carter's office. She knocked and waited. If Carter wouldn't help her, then she would hunt for Jamie on her own.

"Come in." His deep masculine voice came through the door.

"Hi, I need your help." Patti said quickly.

"Have you lost your mind? Why aren't you in the safe house? We agreed for you to stay put," Carter shouted, shock and anger threaded in his tone.

Patti had hoped he would be reasonable. "I won't be bullied. I intend to find Jamie."

He stared at Patti for several long moments. "You're wearing Jamie's hairstyle."

"Do you like it?"

"What are you trying to do? Get yourself killed?"

"Don't yell at me."

"I'm not yelling."

"Your voice sounds very loud to me."

Carter took a breath and asked the question again in a much calmer voice.

"I want to help. I have an idea. Remember when you told me it wasn't safe because I look like Jamie?"

"Of course," he said. "What you're getting at?"

"Just listen to my idea and don't dismiss it." She gave him a look and waited.

Finally, he nodded.

"I want to go where Jamie was working. When the people there see me...who knows, it might rattle a few cages. Something's bound to happen. It's a good idea. It will work."

"A good idea that might get you killed."

"I can't sit and wait. If I can use the fact Jamie and I are identical twins to find her, then I will. With or without your help."

"This isn't a game, Patti."

"Don't you think I know that? It's my sister who's missing."

Carter took a deep breath and drummed his fingers on his desk. "I know it's hard, but you've got to have faith."

"Faith in who?" Her heart raced.

"Faith in me, the FBI, and in God," his voice was soft and low. "Believe me, Patti. I want you to see Jamie again. I want Sabrina to have her mommy back."

"OK, you want me to trust you. Then you need to trust me. I want...no...I need to know what's going on."

"You need to let the professionals handle this situation."

The slip of paper and the key were her ace in the hole. "You don't trust me. Just tell me what city she flies off to all the time. That's all I want to know."

"I do trust you, Patti."

"It sure doesn't feel that way, Carter. I look like Jamie. I can speed the investigation along."

"There's no way Marcus would put you in harm's way. And I'm not even asking him."

"You think Jamie's dead, don't you?" her voice trembled with emotion.

"She's dealing with some very dangerous peop—"

"What people?"

Carter stood and closed the door, and then perched on his desk. "If I tell you, will you go back to the safe house?"

"Tell me what you know."

He stared at her, and then nodded. "This is confidential information. Do not tell anyone or I'll get fired. Jamie's working with an Anti-Terrorist task force in cooperation with Homeland Security."

Stunned, she opened her mouth to speak, but no words came out. Finally, she choked out the words. "Anti-terrorist? I thought this was about drugs."

"We were wrong. Now you know why you need to go back to the safe house and let the FBI handle the situation."

Jamie. Out there with terrorists.

She couldn't breathe and her heart pounded. She breathed deep and gripped deep, hidden strength through sheer willpower.

"I'm not going back, Carter. Just tell me what city she works in." Patti kept her voice calm and reasonable. "If I go there, I could—"

"You can't do that," Carter exploded, on his feet within seconds. "I forbid you."

"You can't forbid me to do anything. This is still America and as far as I know, it's not a police state." Glaring, Patti jumped up. "I can do what I want."

"I'll put you in protective custody," Carter yelled.

"And I'll call the papers and tell them I was detained illegally."

The seconds ticked off.

Patti became aware of Carter's raw masculine energy.

Her stomach turned to butterflies as he moved towards her. When he reached out and touched her arm, Patti felt a stab of disappointment. She'd wanted more from him than a simple touch on the arm—a lot more.

"It won't help Jamie if we are at each other's

throats." Carter flashed his charming smile. "Let's be friends."

"Your kind of friendship, I don't need."

"I'm doing everything I can to keep you safe. Did you hear me say the word, terrorists?"

Terrorists.

This was so much more complex than she'd first believed. Carter was right. There wasn't anything she could do to help Jamie. It was in God's hands.

Patti sat down, relieved to move away from Carter. "I can't believe any of this. Terrorists."

"Well, believe it."

She took the address and key out of her pocket and handed it to him. She wasn't going to jeopardize Jamie's safety to prove a point.

"Anna gave me these. She was afraid to give them to me in front of you so she waited until we got to the safe house. She thought they might be personal. I have no idea what it means. Has to be important, but I don't know what to do with it, or where to start."

"It's too small for a house key. Could it be for a safety deposit box?" He inspected the paper she'd given him. "2057 Southern-Abby Lane #411. No city or state." He looked up and gave her a thoughtful look. "Were you planning to investigate by yourself?"

"Maybe. Did Marcus tell you what city she worked in?"

"You think this address might be in the city where Jamie worked?"

"It's possible. If I could find it..." her words trailed off.

"If I told you where she works, would it prove I trust you?"

"Maybe."

"I can't, Patti. I don't know myself."

"I just...I can't believe this." Patti jumped up from the chair.

"Well, believe it." Carter raised his hands in a gesture of frustration. "You could make the situation worse."

Trust, respect, and cooperation were the things she wanted from him. Their gazes met.

Carter spoke quietly, his eyes never leaving hers. "I know it's frustrating. That little girl may have already lost her mother. She doesn't need to lose her aunt, too." He took a deep breath and touched her arm. "And I care because I...I...think you make the world a better place by being it."

Hokey, but her heart skipped a beat, anyway. Then her practical side took over.

Men used any means to get what they wanted. He wanted Patti to be a good little soldier and go back to the safe house.

She refused to be manipulated. "I thought maybe it was an address here that could help. I wish I'd looked closer at those IDs."

"The FBI took all of them." Carter glanced over at the computer. "I suppose it couldn't hurt to look at an address. We have a program that accesses addresses from across the country. Let's start with Palm Beach. You never know, we might get lucky."

He typed in the address.

NO SUCH ADDRESS flashed on the screen.

"Let's expand the search to within two hundred miles of Palm Beach."

"Good idea." Patti inched forward.

When Carter turned to her and smiled, she realized she was pressed up against him.

She moved back embarrassed. "I was just trying to look—"

"Yeah, I know what you were trying to do."

"Behave, Carter."

They found nothing.

Carter looked up. "Maybe I'll check California."

"Why would you..." A light bulb came on.

He was giving her privileged information.

She wanted to hug him. "Thank you, Carter."

"I know Marcus flew out to California, but not which city. Let's start with the major cities."

They were still searching when a knock startled them. The door opened and a man walked in without waiting for an invitation. He stared, anger making his face appear ruddy.

Patti moved back to her own chair.

"Caldwell, you don't look like you're working on the order I gave you."

"This is Patti Jakowski, Chief. We were just—"

"You're not on the case. There is no case, remember?"

"No case?" Patti asked, her gaze moving between the two men.

The tension between them was obvious.

Carter looked at Patti. "I'll explain later." He turned back to the chief. "We were trying to locate an address. You can't call that investig—"

"I don't care what you call it. I call it investigating, Caldwell."

Patti started to speak, but one look from Carter made her stop.

"You're not on the case, Caldwell because there is no case, as far as we are concerned. I thought I made that clear. Plain and simple. Don't make me have to write you up or worse." He gave Patti a look. "And I suggest you get yourself back to the safe house. I'll have an officer take you."

"I'm not going back."

He slammed the door as he walked out.

17

Patti stared at the closed door for a moment, then back at Carter. "Why is there no case?"

"The FBI took over and told us to butt out."

Carter was off the case, and he hadn't bothered to tell her. "You said you could trust Marcus."

"The FBI are doing all they can to find Jamie. I believe that." He paced around the room, knocking over files and books as he moved. He bent over, picked them up, and tossed them on his desk.

Patti picked up the paper and the key and held them up. "This is where we could start. Jamie wanted me to have this. It must be important."

"It's a big state. It could be anywhere. And we can't find it." Carter perched on the desk in front of Patti. "We're going to have to trust the FBI on this."

"But I can help. Can't you call Marc—"

"How, Patti? What exactly can you do? Pretend to be Jamie, but who and where should you do it? We have no idea where this place is. Speaking of places, how exactly did you get out of the safe house, anyway? And why wasn't I notified you left?"

"I walked out the front door. Anna distracted the men."

Carter clutched his head with one hand. His disgust was evident.

Patti didn't care.

Jamie was involved with people who might kill

her. It was more than Patti could handle. She stood. "You win. I'm leaving."

"I'll drive you back to the safe house."

"No need. I have a rental. Thanks for offering."

"I should take you back."

"Why? Everyone's telling you it's not your case any longer, so you should believe them."

"What are you planning to do?"

"Nothing. Remember I'm not the detective."

"Take care of Sabrina and yourself." Carter took her hand. "I'll contact you if I learn anything. Once this is all over maybe we can spend some time getting to know each other." He leaned over and brushed her cheek with his lips.

His lips were soft and warm, but a chill went down her spine.

"I'm sorry—that was unprofessional of me." Carter moved away from Patti.

There was no need to apologize. None at all.

"Don't be."

She walked out of the air-conditioned police station into the steaminess of a Florida afternoon. She turned back half-expecting to see Carter. Refusing to acknowledge her disappointment, she told herself it was for the best. She touched her cheek. It could hardly be called a kiss, but still...

She got in the car and unfolded the paper. Frustrated, she spoke aloud. "Jamie, why didn't you give me more information? What did you want me to know?" She stared at the address.

2057 Southern-Abby Lane #411.

Her sister wouldn't make it difficult for Patti. It must be in the Palm Beach area, and yet Carter double-checked the address. The address didn't exist in the state of Florida.

She bumped her head on the steering wheel. *Think. Think. Jamie had given her a clue.*

The cell phone rang, causing her to jerk with surprise. By the time she found it, the phone stopped ringing. She flipped it open and hit the send button.

"Hey." Carter seemed to be trying to whisper, yet speak loud enough for her to hear him. "Where are you? I'm not ready to give up on that address quite yet."

"Your boss told you not to investigate any further. I don't want you—"

"I made a promise to you and I always keep my promises to my…my friends." He took a deep breath. "I let my job stop me from doing what was right once, and I'm not going to let it happen again."

Patti's heart and head turned to mush. She looked towards the police station.

The door opened and Carter walked out. He looked around and gave a small wave.

She waved back. *This guy will break my heart if I let him.*

Carter sauntered out to the car.

"Carter, you can't help me. Your boss said—" She said as she got out.

"Don't worry about him. I'm not."

"But…"

"A promise is a promise. Maybe it's time for me to find a different job." He held out his hand. "Now, let me look at the address again."

She handed him the paper. "Jamie obviously thought I wouldn't have any trouble figuring it out."

"Then what are we missing?"

"She assumed I would know where, and that

means Palm Beach, but…"

"The address doesn't exist." Carter finished Patti's sentence.

"Exactly."

"Does Palm Beach have an Abby Lane? Maybe, Jamie was mistaken about the Southern part."

"No, I put Abby Lane in the computer. No Such Address."

"I wonder why she put a dash between Southern and Abby Lane. That's not the usual way to write an address."

Carter looked down at the paper and frowned. "What an idiot I am! I can't believe I didn't see it."

"See what? I don't get it."

"You don't know the city. I do. It's Southern Boulevard, and my guess is Abby Lane is a person who lives there."

"You think?" Patti asked, her voice tinged with doubt.

"Only one way to find out. Let's go take a look."

Southern Boulevard didn't go south at all, but was an east-west road that ran from downtown Palm Beach to the airport and beyond.

"There it is," Patti pointed and yelled when she saw the number on the front of an office building.

"I'll pull into the bus station parking lot. That's a lot easier than trying to find a spot right in front of the building."

Once they parked, Carter and Patti hurried across the street.

An old man hobbled past them, using a cane.

Patti locked gazes with him. Something in his eyes made her shiver, even in the heat.

As they passed, she turned around to get a better

look.

He'd stopped walking and leaned on his cane. His gasping met her ears.

Her paranoia was getting the best of her.

"What's wrong?"

The old man moved down the street at a snail's pace.

"Nothing. Just my imagination going wild."

Patti shivered as they entered the air-conditioned building. It was a wonder the whole state didn't have pneumonia walking in and out of sweltering heat into freezers.

"Right there." Carter pointed at the directory.

It read, Abby Lane, Attorney at Law.

"Makes sense. You know, this was all your fault."

"My fault? How can you say that?"

"This is your city. You should have understood the address when you looked at it." She gave him a playful tap.

They walked towards the elevator.

She glanced back through the glass to the street.

The old man still stood in the street staring at the building. Or was he staring at her?

The ding of the elevator drew her attention.

Carter's eyes narrowed. "Everything ok?"

She nodded.

After leaving the elevator, they walked past a door.

Patti stopped.

"What's wrong?" Carter asked.

She pointed at the sign on the door. "It says J.L. Jakowski. Jamie's middle name is Lynn. This must be Jamie's office."

"I wonder why she needs an office." Carter pulled

out the key. "No way this keys opens that door."

"If that's her office, we need to get in there. Maybe I can ask Abby Lane to let us in."

Carter's cell phone buzzed. He took it out and looked at it. "It's Marcus. They've figured out you aren't where you're supposed to be. And this second call is from my boss. I'd say they definitely know we're both gone."

"What are you going to do?"

"I'm going to ignore them. Like you said, I'm off the case."

"I don't want you getting in—"

He took hold of her elbow. "Don't worry about me. I'm a big boy, and I can take care of my own problems."

"But—"

"No buts, let's go."

They found a door marked Abby Lane.

Patty turned to Carter. "Should I act like I'm Jamie or what?"

"Let's play it by ear. If it looks like it will be the easiest way to find out what the key goes to, then go for it."

They walked into an elegant office.

Four formal Queen Anne chairs were lined against the wall and a matching settee sat on the opposite wall. The furniture was dark cherry wood with an old-fashioned, flower print fabric, making it cheerful.

A receptionist sat at a desk talking on the phone. She held up a hand acknowledging Carter and Patti.

They stood quietly waiting for her to finish the call.

She smiled. Her gaze looked Carter up and down, but then turned back to Patti.

"Hi, Jamie. I wasn't expecting to see you today. What brings you here?"

"Hi," Patti said with a smile. She slid the key out of her pocket and held it up.

"Oh, you need to get in your lockbox. No problem." The woman stood and walked down the hall.

Carter gave Patti a thumbs-up as they followed.

The receptionist stopped at a door with a keypad on it, hit some numbers, and when a light flashed green, opened it.

Unlike the elegant reception area, a simple round table and chairs sat in the room. Built into the walls were rows and rows of numbered lockboxes.

She turned and called back over her shoulder. "Just hit the buzzer when you're ready to leave, Jamie."

"Thanks." Once the door was closed, Patti whispered to Carter. "A lot easier than I thought it would be."

"It's about time something went our way, don't you think?"He pointed at the lockboxes lighting the walls. "I guess we know what the number is for now."

"Let's hope so."

She found number 411. Her hand shook as she slipped the key into the hole. It opened without a problem. There were several envelopes of various sizes.

"This is what we were looking for, but a part of me doesn't want to know."

"Leave them if you want. There's no law saying you have to take them."

But she had to help Jamie.

꙰

A blast of heat slammed into her as they walked out into the blinding sunshine. *How did people get used to this?* Patti clutched the envelopes from the lockbox and turned towards Carter. "I need to be by myself for awhile so I can look at these."

"That's fine. I can find a hotel for you, or we can go to my house. Or you could go back to the safe house. Your choice."

"Your house is fine."

They stopped and waited for the light to turn red.

As she stepped off the curb, Carter put a hand on her elbow and moved closer. His hip touched hers. He leaned down and nuzzled her hair. Stunned by his bold and unexpected action, she stopped moving, but he propelled her forward.

"Don't panic. Someone's following us."

Can't fall apart. Keep walking.

He reached inside his shirt, and in the same moment, pushed her hard enough to make her fall to the ground.

Staring up she saw a gun in his hand.

Patti crawled towards the bushes.

Shots rang out.

18

Patti scrambled and crawled to safety behind a car in the parking lot.

More shots.

She peered out, praying Carter wasn't hurt.

People screamed as they ran away from the gunman.

Carter fell to the ground and rolled in the opposite direction of Patti. He returned fire, but the assailant crouched low, and then turned and ran.

Her heart thudded to a stop as her gaze found the gunman.

It was the old man from the street. The one who'd given her the creeps.

This was her fault. She should have told Carter. When their gazes met, she'd known something was off about the man.

Carter jumped up and chased after the gunman. "Police. Stop."

The gunman fired again.

Carter continued to speed toward him.

A woman walked towards the two, apparently oblivious to the unfolding drama.

Patti watched in horror as the gunman grabbed the pregnant woman.

He spun her, using her as a shield.

Carter stopped running, but kept moving slowly towards the man.

The woman screamed and struggled, but couldn't free herself.

"I'll kill her," the man yelled. He put the gun to the woman's head.

She sobbed.

Carter stopped in his tracks. "Let her go."

"I'll let her go when you back off." The gunman moved backwards, eyeing Carter as he spoke. "If you take one more step I'll shoot her."

Patti held her breath.

The woman sobbed harder.

Carter put his hands up in a surrendering motion.

The assailant dragged her backwards until he was even with the back of the bus station. He shoved the woman forward, shot again, and then disappeared behind the building.

The woman collapsed, sobbing hysterically as she held her stomach.

Patti ran to them. "Go ahead. I'll take care of her."

Carter ran off in the same direction as the gunman.

Patti put her arms around the woman. She heard the wail of the police sirens as they approached.

"It's OK. He's gone. You're safe, now." Patti stared at the spot where Carter disappeared.

"Why did he do that to me?"

"I don't know, but God sure was watching over us."

The woman touched her swollen belly and nodded through her tears.

The police converged on the area.

Patti and the woman were helped to an ambulance.

An EMT worker slapped a blood pressure cuff on Patti while an officer asked her questions.

She answered the best she could, but her gaze stayed glued to the spot where Carter disappeared.

After an eternity, Carter came around the corner—alone.

Patti jumped up and rushed over to him.

A sense of safety and sanity returned as his arms tightened around her. She snuggled in closer, savoring the feeling.

Carter was alive.

She breathed deeply, but it turned into a sob as she exhaled.

Carter's hand brushed over her head.

Leaning against him, she allowed her head to fall against his chest.

They stood that way for what seemed like hours.

Finally, she took a small step backwards and looked up at him with a teary smile. "I was so scared. I thought he'd shot you."

"I couldn't catch him," Carter told her, failure in his voice.

"It doesn't matter as long as you didn't get hurt. I was sure he was going...never mind. I'm glad you're safe." Patti was trying not to cry. "It was all my fault. I saw that old man on the street and something seemed off. I should have known."

With those words, he broke the bear hug he'd held Patti in. "Where are the envelopes? Did you lose them in all that craziness?"

She took a few more steps back, embarrassed by her display of emotion. She'd been so glad to see Carter she'd done what seemed natural. "I dropped them, but one of the cops gathered them up for me. They're back at the ambulance."

"Good. Let me go talk with the officer in charge

and then we need to get out of here." He flashed a grin at her. "Before my boss gets here."

Patti stared at the pandemonium around her, but she only had one thing on her mind.

What would those papers tell her about her sister?

19

They pulled into Carter's drive.

His house was a small blue bungalow in desperate need of paint. Flower beds adorned the front of the house but as they walked up, Patti could see as many weeds as flowers. The house was actually surrounded by a white picket fence.

It made her smile.

The moment Patti entered the house her gaze was drawn to the mantle above a fireplace where a huge portrait of Carter and his bride hung.

Her heart sank.

He was married.

It hadn't occurred to her he might have a wife. Her stomach clenched in a knot, remembering the closeness they'd shared only minutes before. And the thoughts and feelings she'd had when he nuzzled her neck. A wave of nausea took her breath away.

"That's Nancy." Carter's voice was soft. "She died a few years ago. In the line of duty. She was a police officer, too."

Waves of relief, immediately followed by guilt, flooded her. "Oh, Carter, I'm so sorry." Patti walked closer to examine the picture.

His bride's long flowing black hair made a sharp contrast to the traditional white gown she wore. Her eyes sparkled with love and happiness.

"She was beautiful."

"She never thought so." His voice was tinged with sorrow. "Nancy always said she wasn't a girly girl. That's why I love this picture. She told me she felt like Cinderella on our wedding day." His green eyes clouded for a moment, but he smiled as looked at Patti. "Of course, she was beautiful every day, but she wouldn't believe me. Always said I was biased."

"It must have been horrible when she died."

"It was. I was so angry when it happened. Angry at everyone. Angry at the killer, angry at my boss, angry at God, but mostly angry at myself for not being able to keep her safe. I lost myself in my anger."

"I'm sure it t wasn't your fault, Carter."

"I've come to accept that. Nancy loved being a cop, and she wouldn't have been happy doing anything else. Except for being a mother, but it wasn't in the cards for us."

He flashed a grin, but the sadness remained in his eyes. He walked around the living room picking up the newspapers tossed on the sofa and gathered up a coffee cup and plate, as well. When he turned back to her the smile in his eyes had returned. "Are you hungry? Want something to drink?"

"I could use a soda."

"Sit down and relax. You've had quite the day."

"That's for sure. It's not every day I get shot at."

"Good thing, huh?" he said as he walked out to the kitchen.

Patti flopped down on the sofa. She laid the envelopes on the coffee table. Her left foot and leg quivered. Pressing down on her leg didn't stop the shaking. Opening what Jamie left for her would be an admission-one she didn't want to face.

She lowered her head to her knees. Tears slid

down her cheeks.

Oh, Jamie, where are you? How could I have wasted so much time being angry? I just want you back. I forgive you, really I do.

How was she supposed to go on living if Jamie was...was...gone?

She'd had years to forgive her, but hadn't. Now, she might never have the chance.

Patti wiped away the tears and picked up the envelopes with trembling hands. Dates were marked on each one. The earliest was legal-sized. The last was addressed to her in Jamie's handwriting.

She held it a long time. Finally, she set it back on the coffee table.

Carter walked in carrying a tray with two plates, two bowls, and two glasses of lemonade.

"Here," he told her as he sat the tray on the coffee table. "You need to eat something."

Tomato soup and a toasted cheese sandwich. It reminded her of childhood lunches...and Jamie. Her eyes filled with tears at his kindness. A wave of emotion threatened to overwhelm her. Her body shook.

"Are you OK, Patti?"

She couldn't talk.

He sat down and his arms went around her. "It's OK. You're having a reaction to what happened. It's normal." He spoke in a calm reassuring tone. "Come here."

She moved closer to him. Unexpected sobs rose up from deep inside her. He held her close and talked in soothing tones as she cried. When the storm passed, Patti looked up and gave him a watery smile.

His hand moved slowly to her face and made its

way down her cheek in a gentle caress that made her heart yearn for more.

She wasn't exhausted or overwhelmed any longer.

Fingers glided down her neck and came to rest on her shoulder.

Their eyes met and he pulled her close.

Patti was powerless to break eye contact or to move away from Carter. Her only desire was...

Carter's mouth covered hers in a sweet, gentle kiss.

Her eyes closed, savoring the moment. She smelled citrus mixed with his own masculine scent, and tasted the tanginess of the lemonade on his lips. The gentle kiss turned to passion. Like waves sweeping the ocean floor, she let the emotions flow.

Patti moved her head slightly and as their lips parted the spell was broken.

Carter took a deep breath.

In spite of her anxiety over Jamie, a part of her wanted to sing.

He pointed at the food. "If you don't eat something, you're going to pass out any minute. You need to listen to Dr. Caldwell."

She smiled and gave him a salute. "Yes, sir."

Small talk evaporated as they finished lunch.

Patti couldn't avoid it any longer. With shaky hands and a heavy heart, Patti picked up the brown envelope. She pulled out the papers and scanned them. A will.

She gulped back the tears and handed it to Carter without reading it.

Opening the next, several documents fell out. One was an insurance policy with Sabrina listed as the beneficiary. The second was a typed list of bank accounts with numbers and locations. In the margin, she'd listed names.

Patti assumed the names listed were the beneficiary of the accounts. Patti's name was on a majority of the accounts, but Anna was listed on several, as well.

After she read each paper, she passed them to Carter.

Finally, there was only one left.

Patti's whole body trembled. She closed her eyes and bowed her head.

"I'll give you some privacy. I'll be outside in the back if you need me."

She nodded, but said nothing. Minutes passed before she picked up the letter. She unfolded it. Her eyes blurred. The words ran together. She touched the handwritten note.

Jamie had written these words to her.

She wiped away the tears and focused on the words.

Dear Patti,

First of all, let me say I love you. I haven't done a very good job of showing you lately, but know that it is true. I do love you. I'm sorry I have been such a rotten sister. I didn't mean to be. Life just got in the way.

Patti couldn't believe it.

Jamie apologizing to her when it should have been the other way around.

I pray that as you read this, my precious daughter, Sabrina, is safely in your arms and your heart. Sabrina is a wonderful little girl and the light of my life. Having Sabrina was the best thing I've ever done. Take care of her and love her, and tell her that her mommy loved her very, very much.

Sabrina's father doesn't know about her. Please don't ever let him know. It wouldn't be safe for her or for you.

He is rich and powerful and has friends who can and will hurt anyone who gets in their way.

I guess if you're reading this, it means things didn't work out exactly the way I wanted. So by now, you probably know I got myself into another mess and this one was a doozey, sis.

I'm not sure how it all happened but I ended up being involved with some unsavory characters years ago. The FBI gave me a choice. I could help them or I could get arrested. I helped them arrest and convict these people. I thought that would be the end, but it wasn't. I was pretty good at the undercover thing, so they gave me some training and I helped them a few more times.

Several months ago, I decided I was being unfair to Sabrina's father (Of course, I didn't know then what I know now.) Anyway, I went looking for him. Before I could tell him about Sabrina, I overheard information that made me suspicious. I couldn't let innocent people die. I had to try and stop it.

All I need to do is find out the ringleader's name, and then the FBI and Homeland can take over. So far, I haven't been successful but I hope to know the name of the ringleader soon.

As soon as I do, I'm coming home. I stayed away from you because it was safer for you, and not for any reasons you may be thinking.

Patti, please don't be hard on yourself. I know you love me. You are probably feeling guilty right now, but don't. You may think it was you who kept us from having a relationship the past several years but it wasn't. It was me *and my job.*

I know with every fiber of my being that had I come to you, you would have forgiven me, so stop feeling guilty.

Patti's tears turned to sobs as she read those words. When she regained her composure, Patti turned back to the letter.

The fact you are reading this letter means something went wrong. I can only assume my lawyer has been in touch with you and that's how you got this letter. I wrote this to explain that I was trying to do my best. I was trying to do what was right.

Please forgive me for all my shortcomings as a sister. I know I haven't been there for you the way I should have been, but I have tried to be the best mother I could to Sabrina. And I'm trying to do the right thing for my country.

I want you to know I have found the most wonderful relationship. This relationship has given me strength and peace and joy. This relationship has sustained me like no other. No matter what I endured in the last moments of my life, don't be too sad. I have found a personal relationship with my Savior and know that I'm with Him at this very moment.

Tears flooded Patti's eyes again, but not from sadness.

Peace descended.

I know you will grieve for me, but don't get stuck in that grief. Life is a wonderful thing and shouldn't be wasted on too much sadness. Patti, I know you will take wonderful care of Sabrina. Please let her know that her mommy loved her so very much.

All my love,
Jamie

P.S. I'm sure the lawyer told you about my apartment in San Francisco at 1500 Santé Fe Boulevard. All you need to do is call the management and tell them I no longer need the apartment. It's all been arranged and they will take care of everything, but someone needs to let them know.

I'm sorry I wasn't the sister I should have been. Please take care of Sabrina and tell her that I love her. And know that I will see you again.

Patti felt a chill go up her spine. It was as if her sister was talking to her from the grave.

20

Carter sat at a patio table talking on the phone.

Green patches of grass mixed with brown sand dotted the landscape. The ocean was just on the horizon.

Patti took in the view, noting fluffy clouds and bright blue sky. Heat shimmered.

"I know, Marcus. It's too bad I couldn't catch him. He just disappeared. The man is obviously a pro. His disguise fooled me. Each time, he looked completely different. Who knows what the man really looks like." A pause. "Patti's fine, but shaken up."

She tapped him on the shoulder. "I want to talk to Marcus."

Carter looked up.

Her heart thumped at his expression.

He nodded in acknowledgement and grabbed her hand.

She moved closer and in one swift movement, he maneuvered her to his lap.

He hit the speakerphone button and interrupted Marcus's tirade. "Marcus, Patti wants to talk with you."

As much as she enjoyed where she was sitting, Patti stood and moved away from Carter. "I have an idea. I want you to send me to the people whom Jamie was dealing with. My showing up will shock them so much it will bring the leader out of hiding and I'll be able—"

Carter exploded. "No way, Marcus. There's no way that's going to happen."

Marcus was yelling the same thing to her from the other side of the phone.

"Just listen to…"

She tossed the phone on the table. "I am going to do this. She may have…have…" Patti took a deep breath and said the words she'd been avoiding. "She may have… I'm not going to let her die in vain. I can find out who the man is and I'm going—"

The two men took turns telling her why she couldn't do it.

She tuned them out. Her mind was made up.

Carter hung up the phone. "Patti, I know you wanted to…"

"I can't believe you took Marcus's side. I need to help Jamie. I would think you, of all people, would understand that. Wouldn't you have done anything to keep your wife safe?"

"There's no way I'm going to help you get yourself killed. Nancy and Jamie were trained to handle themselves and things still went wrong. You're not trained. It's far too dangerous. You wouldn't have a chance."

The argument grew more heated. He didn't care about her or he'd understand she had to do this—for Jamie.

"I need to go."

"Patti, let's get this settled. I don't want this to affect our…our –" Carter searched for the word.

Patti forced her thoughts back to her sister.

Carter said he wanted to help her find Jamie. Now

he was arguing against that. He'd kissed her a few minutes before, perhaps trying to make her forget her quest?

She stared at him, her heart breaking. "I'm exhausted. I need to go to a hotel and get some rest. It's been a really bad day."

"You can rest here for a while." Carter offered. "Or you can go back to the safe house."

"No, I want to go to a hotel, and you need to return to the station before you lose your job."

"That doesn't matter."

"It matters, Carter. Go talk with your boss."

"Fine, I'll take you to a hotel and get a cab. You get a few hours sleep and when I'm done, we'll go out for dinner, later."

"No, I want to go to a hotel by myself. I need to be alone."

"Patti, don't shut me out."

She turned away from him. "I just need...need to rest."

On the drive to the hotel, Carter attempted to talk, but she remained quiet. There was nothing left to say

He drove around until they were sure they hadn't been followed. Then he took her to a nice hotel.

As they were about to get on the elevator, Patti turned with a sad smile. "Thanks, Carter. I can take it from here." She stepped on the elevator alone and went to her room.

With or without Carter's help, Patti knew what she had to do.

∂∽⧉

Carter stormed around his house picking up

dishes and other clutter. What an idiot he was! He'd blown it with Patti. He'd seen it on her face when he didn't stand up for her against Marcus. He'd failed the test. But all he wanted to do was keep Patti safe—if she'd let him.

The look in her eyes when he'd left her at the hotel...Patti felt betrayed...by him.

Carter tossed the cup in the sink. He heard the sound of breaking glass. *Oh, great.* He couldn't even do the dishes right. Picking up the broken pieces of the cup, he threw them in the trash much harder than necessary. He stomped back into the living room.

Patti had been sweet, kind, and understanding, as he talked about Nancy.

He stared up at the picture for a long time, remembering two women...Nancy...and Patti...

"Nancy, I loved you and I still do, but it's time to put away the past." He reached up to take the picture down, but hesitated.

Not yet.

With a sigh, he put the picture back. He hoped Patti understood the next time she came--if there was a next time.

By morning, she'd realize how dangerous it would be to go into the lion's den, so to speak. Patti was smart. She'd figure that out on her own. He reached for the phone but decided against it. They needed a cooling off period. Then they could talk in a more reasonable way. He'd call her first thing in the morning.

Then they could come up with a plan.

21

San Francisco, California

Patti's taxi turned off Fillmore onto a side street, leaving behind the bustle of business for the more tranquil residential area of Pacific Heights.

It was one of the trendier areas of San Francisco, the cab driver told her.

The streets were lined with chic boutiques, elegant cafes, and high-priced condos.

Patti ran fingers through her new haircut, then stopped. She wasn't Patti, the school guidance counselor, any longer. She was Jamie, always confident, always charming, and always the center of attention. If she was to be successful with this deception, she must think like Jamie—not Patti. And she had no choice but to succeed.

Her first act of deception would be to get a key to Jamie's apartment. She hoped she could pull off the charade that long.

Carter would go ballistic if he knew what she was up to. He'd pretended to be someone she could count on, but when she'd needed him most...Patti shook her head as if that would erase Carter from her thoughts.

She had only one job to do—find Jamie.

Swallowing back her tears, she paid the cab driver. She stepped out of the taxi and sauntered towards the door in true Jamie fashion. It opened as if by magic.

A short bald man with a big smile stepped out of the building. Although he wore a cream-colored linen suit instead of a traditional uniform, Patti assumed by his demeanor he was the doorman. He looked to be in his early forties but it was hard to be sure. His bald head glistened in the last fading sunlight of the day.

"Ms. Jakowski, you're back. I was beginning to believe you were never coming home." His smile seemed genuine to Patti. He must like Jamie.

"It was a long trip this time." Patti smiled back at the man. So far, so good.

"That's for sure."

Jamie would have used his name, but since she couldn't she gave him her best Jamie smile. "I can't tell you how glad I am to be back. How are things?"

The man's smile disappeared and he leaned in close. His voice was a whisper. "Two FBI agents were here looking for you. Is everything Ok? They had a warrant and made me take them up to your apartment. I tried to stay and see what happened, but they sent me on my merry way."

Her heart pounded.

The FBI.

Of course, Marcus would have searched Jamie's apartment.

Stay calm.

Patti desperately tried to think of an answer to satisfy the waiting man. "Did they tell you anything?"

"No." The man shook his head. "Just asked about you and went to your apartment, but they didn't mess anything up. I checked afterwards to make sure everything was OK. Tomas was very agitated by the whole matter."

Who was Tomas? This was getting more

complicated by the moment. She would never be able to pull to this charade off. She flashed a Jamie smile at the man. "Don't worry about it. You did what you had to do. Everything is just fine." Patti stepped in and spoke in a hushed confidential tone. "The FBI was looking for missing files from my company. They checked every one of the employees. It wasn't personal." Patti hoped her answer made sense.

His bald head was nodding up and down.

So far, so good.

"Of course, of course. I knew it was something like that. I knew you'd never do anything illegal."

Inwardly, she breathed a small sigh of relief. One bullet down. Patti wondered how many more bullets were heading in her direction. She gave him a meaningful look. "Everything's marvelous. No need to worry. They didn't ask you to call them when I came home, did they?"

He looked aghast at the suggestion that he might call the FBI on her. "They did, but I always respect tenant privacy, you know that. Where's your luggage?"

Anna had told her Jamie never took luggage with her. Time to improvise. She sighed with exaggeration.

Jamie had been known as The Drama Queen in high school.

"You know the airlines. Which brings me to another problem. I can't get in the apartment. My keys were in my luggage."

"We haven't used keys in years, but I know what you mean. Don't worry about it. It will only take a minute to get you another card. I'll be right back."

As the man left, Patti rubbed her temples. Her nerves were as taut as if she were living the nightmare of showing up at school for her job, but hadn't done that year's scheduling. Terrifying.

The lobby had two elegant Victorian chairs. A dark, shiny mahogany end table between the chairs sat on a small Persian rug. Off to the side was a reception counter and a door.

Looking around, she found three elevators. She knew some elevators were programmed to only go to certain floors. Hopefully, she would pick the right one.

The doorman rushed towards her with his hands full of mail. As he handed her the mail and the key card, panic set in.

She didn't know Jamie's apartment number. She looked down at the mail, but the address didn't show a number. Obviously, residents shared a main street address and picked up their mail at the front desk.

With a flash of brilliance, Patti let the card slip from her grip. With another exaggerated sigh, she smiled at the doorman.

He bent to pick up the key card.

"Be a dear and ride up with me. My hands are full."

"Certainly, Ms. Jakowski."

The doorman walked to the elevator on the far right side. He put the keycard into a slot.

The elevator door slid open.

They stepped inside.

He looked at her and she smiled back though her heart was racing.

How was she going to know which button to hit? Her pulse quickened. She waited to see what floor he would choose, but was surprised to see no numbers announcing the floors.

He slipped the key card into another slot Patti

hadn't noticed. The elevator quietly started its upward climb.

Of course, everything Jamie did was first class. The penthouse apparently had its own private elevator.

"Did anyone else come looking for me besides the FBI?" Patti asked, with what she hoped was nonchalance.

"Just Mr. Hamed. I told him you weren't here, but he does have his own key card so..." The man held up his hands in mock surrender. "He went into your apartment but didn't stay long." The look on his face told her he didn't exactly approve of Mr. Hamed.

"Did Mr. Hamed come before, or after the FBI?"

"Mmmm." The man tapped his head as if to jog the memory loose. "It seems to me he came after the FBI, but I'm not sure."

"Did you tell him the FBI had been here?"

"Certainly not. It wasn't my place."

The elevator stopped.

He slid the key card in yet another slot.

The elevator doors slid open revealing a spacious apartment, not a hallway.

Patti managed to hide her surprise.

She smiled at the doorman. "It sure is nice to be back home."

"Traveling is OK, but the best part is always coming home, don't you think?" He chuckled.

"Isn't that the truth?" She thanked the doorman as he handed her the key card.

"I'll let Tomas know you're back."

"Hold on a minute." She reached for her purse.

A look of surprise crossed his face and he waved her away. "That's OK, Ms. Jakowski. You take good care of me. I don't need anything extra."

Another faux pas.

The doorman walked to the elevator, but then stopped and turned back to Patti. "Are you sure everything's OK? You seem different."

"I'm just exhausted." No lies or deception there. It was the truth. She felt as if she might collapse at any moment.

He nodded with understanding. "Well, don't worry about a thing. Perhaps, you want me to wait until the morning to place those calls."

"No, no, go ahead." She had no idea what he meant, but acted as if she did. "That would be fantastic."

He stepped on the elevator.

As the elevator doors closed, she crumpled to the floor.

22

Patti sat on the floor, hugging her knees to her chest. That hadn't gone well at all. Even Jamie's doorman hadn't been fooled. If she couldn't deceive him, how could she expect anyone to believe she was Jamie?

Her breathing quickened and her pulse raced. *Oh, no. Not now.* She knew the symptoms of an anxiety attack well enough to recognize them. *No time to fall apart. Breathe.* With each slow deliberate breath, her body relaxed a bit more.

After a few moments, she was able to stand up. Staring around the room, she shook her head.

Jamie had a knack for the dramatic when it came to decorating. It was as amazing as Jamie's house in Florida.

She stood in the center of one huge room. A combination of living room, dining room and kitchen, though a counter did separate the kitchen from the other areas.

The furnishings were expensive and elegant like at Jamie's house, but instead of traditional, they were sleek and modern. A wall of windows formed one side of the apartment.

In front of the bank of windows, Jamie had arranged a loveseat, a chair, and a small table.

Patti walked over and stared out at the city. It gave

her the unnerving feeling of open space, but it was spectacular.

The summer sun was dropping down over the horizon, casting orange, yellow and red hues across the evening sky. The twinkling city lights mixed with the sunset.

Down below, she could see the shimmering water.

Awesome.

How many times had Jamie stood in that same spot, lonely and vulnerable, wishing she could talk with Patti?

Patti's eyes filled with tears. Her sister had needed her, and she hadn't been there for her. She'd been too self-absorbed, and brooding about the past.

She turned her back on the sunset.

On the right side of the room was a stone fireplace.

Her gaze moved up to the mantel.

The Picasso, again.

She touched it.

A print this time. Definitely not the original.

Staring at the image, Patti wondered what it had meant to Jamie. Two sides of the same person? Or a deeper meaning, a dark twin and a light twin? And if that was the case, which was she? A week ago, the self-righteous Patti would have known the answer, but now — not so much.

Turning around, she gazed at the rest of the apartment. The dining area had chairs and a table with elegant tiles forming a motif on the top. Stainless steel appliances made up the third wall. A U-shaped bar separated the kitchen from the living and dining areas, but it still gave the feeling of being one room.

She didn't know what to do, now that she was actually standing inside Jamie's apartment.

Her stomach growled. She walked over to the refrigerator and opened it. Empty. Which made sense.

Jamie hadn't been here in at least two weeks from what Patti could figure out.

She could call for a pizza to be delivered, but wasn't sure of the procedure for ordering food.

The doorman was already suspicious.

This didn't quite look like the place where a lot of pizzas were delivered, more likely sushi or some other exotic food.

She decided against ordering take-out. It was far too risky.

If she'd been thinking, she'd have eaten before she came to the apartment building. Then again, if she'd been thinking, she wouldn't have come to San Francisco at all.

Carter would be furious when he found out.

If he found out, she corrected herself.

She had no obligation to–a buzzer interrupted her thoughts.

Feeling like a student who'd been summoned to the principal's office, the panic set in once again. What was she supposed to do? Spying a phone beside the elevator, she walked over and lifted up the receiver. "Hello?"

"Ms. Jakowski." It was the voice of the doorman. "Your grocery order is here."

Her mouth opened to say she hadn't ordered anything, but she closed it just as quickly. She wasn't sure how or why food was being magically delivered, but decided it was a good thing. She was starving. "Great. Send it up."

Moments later another buzzer sounded, but this one had a different tone than the intercom. She pressed the single button under the phone, hoping it was the right thing to do.

The elevator door opened. A teenage girl with long brown hair walked out carrying several plastic bags in both hands. She wore a T-shirt and faded jeans. A Bluetooth was stuck in one ear and an I-Pod earpiece in the other.

"Hey, Jamie," the girl said with a bright smile, walking towards the kitchen.

"Hi." Patti tagged along.

The girl seemed to know what she was doing so Patti stood back and let her do her job. The young woman pulled out the earpiece and looked at Patti.

"Wow! You were sure gone a long time."

"Yeah, work ended up taking longer than planned. I'm glad to be back, though."

The girl gave Patti a quizzical look, but said nothing. She stopped at the kitchen island and set the bags on it.

Patti walked over trying to look more interested.

The girl seemed to expect it.

"So, guess who asked me out for next weekend?" The delivery girl asked in a gossipy tone as she handed Patti a sales slip.

Patti had no idea what to say, or what to do with the sales slip.

It seemed obvious Jamie and this girl had more of a relationship than just delivery girl to her customer.

She shrugged, not knowing what to say. She forced herself to sound interested and gossipy. "I don't know."

The girl's sparkle dissipated, her shoulders dropped, and she looked crestfallen.

Patti tried to repair the situation as best she could.

"Well, tell me."

"Never mind. Can you sign the slip or do you want to check it first?" she snapped at Patti. This girl wasn't happy with Patti's imitation of Jamie.

"No, don't be silly. I trust you." Patti looked around for a pen and spied one sitting on the counter by the phone. She picked up the pen and signed the slip.

"So, come on, tell me your big news." Patti tried to sound chummy as she handed the delivery girl back the signed receipt.

The girl took the receipt without looking at it. She didn't answer Patti's question. Instead, she asked her own question. "Are you all right, Jamie?"

"Sure. Why do you ask?" Patti felt sweat forming on her hands. She rubbed them against her jeans. The feel of the denim against her hands made her question whether Jamie would choose to wear jeans while being undercover, or would she have chosen something more elegant. Too late, now.

"I don't know. You seem different."

Of course, she was different. She didn't have the first idea how to act like Jamie. When they'd been young, they'd been able to fool their friends, but that was when they both knew all the same people.

She forced a smile. "No, I'm not OK," Patti told the girl. "I'm exhausted from the trip and I've had some bad news. I didn't mean to hurt your feelings. Why don't you sit down and tell me what's going on in your life?" Patti went to her purse and got a five, and then changed her mind and chose two twenties instead.

The girl considered Patti's offer for a moment. "Nah, that's OK. Like you said, you're tired. I'll tell you later." She reached out her hand for the tip.

"Thanks for the money. It goes right into the college fund."

"Good idea."

Confusion crossed the girl's face once again.

Patti ignored the look and decided to get some information. "You know the doorman, right?"

"Sure."

"Did he call you?"

"Sure, Robert or Tomas always calls us when you get in and then I bring over your standing order. That's what you wanted me to do, right?"

"Absolutely," Patti answered lamely, searching her mind for a reason to ask such an odd question. "I just wondered if Robert was still working, that's all. I needed to ask him something."

"Oh, do you want me to send him up?"

"No, no. I'll check with him later."

After the girl left, Patti couldn't shake the feeling she failed her second test as Jamie. But at least she now knew the doorman's name. If she couldn't do any better, she'd better give up the charade and go home.

The moment the thought popped in her head, she knew it was the right thing to do. She had no business being in San Francisco. How could she find Jamie when the professionals couldn't?

She sat down on the nearest bar stool, exhausted and overwhelmed. Her heart beat faster and the air in the apartment pushed in on her. Sweat pooled in the palms of her hands. Her self-controlled slipped away. Her breathing quickened and she knew it was a matter of moments before she had an all-out panic attack.

No.

Taking a deep breath, she wouldn't allow it. She'd come to Jamie's apartment for a reason and she'd see it through. It wasn't the time to fall apart like some wimpy girl. Taking slow deep breaths, calmness returned.

It had been hours since she'd eaten the tomato soup and toasted cheese sandwich at Carter's house. At the thought of Carter and his soup, she teared up. Her blood sugar must be low.

Patti opened the refrigerator and grabbed a container the grocery girl delivered. It was some sort of expensive shrimp dip. She found some gourmet crackers in the cupboard and downed several in quick succession. The dip was delicious, but she didn't take the time to enjoy it. She got a bottle of sparkling water out of the fridge and took several long drinks from it.

She spied a door in the kitchen. It led to a hallway.

The first door opened up to Jamie's bedroom.

Another gorgeous view.

Everything was spotless in the room, just like the rest of the apartment. Either Jamie had a good cleaner or she'd changed beyond recognition

Patti checked drawers and closets. She left the room and went to another.

Jamie's office.

Certainly, she'd find phone numbers or addresses of the people Jamie knew.

Patti went to the computer. She turned it on. The cursor flickered, waiting for the password. She typed in Sabrina and it finished booting up.

Her triumph turned to defeat as she realized if there had been anything important on the computer, the FBI would have taken it with them.

She made a face at the computer, but looked at the files, anyway. When her eyes couldn't focus any longer, she came to the conclusion there was nothing to be learned.

So exhausted she could barely move, she stumbled from the chair to the sofa. Her mind wouldn't slow down enough to let her relax.

They'd been so close once. They'd known everything about the other, their thoughts, their feelings, their hopes and dreams. How had she and Jamie come to this point?

Unbidden, a memory came to Patti.

Jamie had sneaked out and gone to the gravel pit to swim with friends.

The boys claimed it was a skinny-dipping party.

Rumors abounded at school.

Jamie swore to Patti and her parents she hadn't gotten naked, no matter what the boys said. Jamie went because her girlfriend insisted on going, and Jamie didn't want her friend to be the only girl. Boys, beer, and one girl were a bad combination.

Patti hadn't stood up for Jamie at school, or with her parents. Instead, she'd distanced herself because she hadn't wanted to ruin her reputation.

Jamie didn't worry about her reputation. She'd always been willing to break the rules if it meant helping someone.

Patti saw it happen more than once when Jamie took the blame and the punishment.

After that incident, Jamie changed.

Patti now understood it had been a turning point.

They began to go their separate ways. Different friends and different activities.

Jamie started saying if she had the reputation, she might as well have the fun to go along with it.

And through it all, Patti hadn't defended her.

Being the wild child and the rebel was what

brought Jamie here to this apartment in San Francisco.

All of it was Patti's fault. If she hadn't been so afraid of what others thought, she would have defended Jamie.

And that could have made all the difference.

23

Palm Beach, Florida

Carter slammed the phone down. He'd waited all night before calling Patti at the hotel. It had been hard, but he wanted her to know he respected her and her needs.

The front desk had informed him Ms. Jakowski checked out the night before, soon after registering.

Not good.

He blew out the anger and took a deep breath, counting slowly. He stopped at two. Maybe, she'd gone back to the safe house.

Could Patti have found out where Jamie went on her business trips?

His stomach turned to acid.

They hadn't gotten around to discussing the letter from Jamie.

It was clear Patti felt betrayed when he sided with Marcus.

He had a bad feeling.

Carter needed to call Marcus, but it was early in California. Marcus would be able to access the airline records to see if Patti had flown to California, as he suspected.

His mood darkened.

Before her death, his wife hadn't listened to reason, either. She'd been fiercely independent, and he had begged her more than once to quit the force and find a safer job. Several years ago she'd made a routine traffic stop. Only it wasn't routine. When she'd called in the tag numbers, she'd discovered the car was wanted as part of an Amber Alert.

The dispatcher told her to wait for backup, but she didn't.

Nancy probably saw the little girl's head pop up from the back seat and wouldn't have taken the chance of the perp driving off.

Nancy and the perp died.

The little girl was in the back seat, hysterical, but healthy.

His wife was trumpeted as a hero, but that didn't make Carter any less alone.

The familiar pain threatened. He'd been an agnostic, but Nancy had been a devout Christian.

A friend pointed out since he was so mad at God for Nancy's death, it must mean he believed in God. That had been the beginning of his journey to find God and peace.

At least until he'd met Patti Jakowski.

He called her cell phone. No answer.

Carter paced his living room, frustrated and angry. On his fourth trip around his furniture, he spied the envelopes, still on his coffee table.

The letter.

Jamie must've left a message for Patti, telling her where to go in California.

Guilt assailed him as he unfolded the note. Was it an invasion of privacy to read it? No, she left it right there. He was a cop, it was his job to protect her. And if she was in danger, then he needed all the information he could use to help Patti. Within minutes, he was on his way to the airport.

Carter booked a flight to San Francisco. He called information and had them put him through to the FBI office in San Francisco. He had to talk with Marcus.

Marcus would be able to keep Patti safe and he could smooth the way with Carter's boss.

"This is Sergeant Carter Caldwell of the Palm Beach Florida Police Department. I'd like to speak to Agent Marcus Hanks."

"There is no Agent Hanks working at this office, sir."

"I know, but he's working out of your office on a special assignment."

"As I said, sir, we have no one by that name who works in this office."

"We're working on a case together and it's crucial I talk with him, now." Carter said. "Can you give him a message?"

"If he checks in, I'll give him the message."

"Please tell him Carter Caldwell called and Patti is somewhere in San Francisco. I'm on my way. On second thought, here's my cell number, just tell him to call me." He ended the call.

While he waited for his flight, Carter tried Patti's cell phone. He left a message asking her to contact him and to stay away from Jamie's apartment.

With a few minutes between flights, he checked for messages from Patti or Marcus. Nothing.

As he rushed to the next gate, he rang Patti again and left a second message. "Please call me, Patti. I need to know you're OK."

When he boarded, the plane taxied along the airway, and then stopped.

After twenty minutes the pilot's voice came on.

"Good morning, there are a few thunderstorms along our flight route. We're waiting for them to pass and then we can get this trip underway."

A collective moan went through the plane.

"I want to go back to the gate," yelled a passenger."I can drive to California faster."

One attendant grabbed the microphone. Her voice was firm, as if speaking to a group of naughty third graders."I know you're all upset, but we need to stay calm. We've been assured it won't be much longer. Please remain in your seats."

The hairs on the back of Carter's neck rose. His gut instinct was screaming.

Patti was in danger.

24

San Francisco, California

Patti awoke with a jerk. Her back and neck hurt from the odd position she'd fallen asleep in on Jamie's sofa. Exhaustion, both physical and emotional, had taken its toll.

Her heart ached in a way she hadn't believed possible. In all likelihood, Patti would never see her twin again. Patti leaned over and held her stomach. She took several deep breaths, trying to ease the pain. She looked at the clock, shocked at the time. She needed to get up and get out of San Francisco.

After Patti cleaned up, she walked around the apartment looking for any momentos Sabrina might want, but nothing caught her eye. Her gaze flickered on the Picasso print. She'd buy her own copy.

Time to leave. Tears threatened, but she refused to indulge in them. She walked towards the elevator. She heard the thump as it came to rest.

Her heart dropped to the pit of her stomach. Who could it be?

Another delivery? If that were the case, Robert or Tomas would have announced them.

She waited for the buzz requesting entrance, but instead the elevator door opened and a dark-haired man rushed towards her.

He moved so fast, she had no time to react.

He held her in his arms, speaking in a language she didn't recognize. He alternated between hugging her tightly, and then caressing her hair. He took her face in both of his hands and kissed her cheeks, her eyelids, her nose, her mouth. He spoke endearments she didn't understand.

As this stranger held her, she realized just how truly stupid she'd been. There was no way she could make anyone think she was Jamie, especially Jamie's lover. How was she supposed to fool this man who knew Jamie in such an intimate way?

Patti didn't even know his name.

Did Jamie speak his language? What would he expect from her? Her mind made a jump to a place she had no desire to go. She shut down the thought. Instead, she focused on what she was going to do in the next five minutes.

Patti's heart raced and every muscle in her body tensed. Forcing her muscles to relax, she took a small step backwards and smiled up at the stranger who still embraced her.

"Jamie, Jamie. I have missed you so much. You were supposed to be back much sooner. I have phoned you many times, but you did not answer. I was worried about you. I left you many messages. Why didn't you call me the moment you got in? When did you get in?" His perfect English had a slight accent.

She heard Jamie's voice in her head.

Calm down and relax. You can do this. Think like me.

"I got in last night, but I was so exhausted I didn't check the messages on my phone here and my cell phone broke. You wouldn't believe the time I've had." Patti lowered her tone to sound more like Jamie.

His hands were still on both sides of her head and

the only thing Patti could think of was he could snap her neck in the blink of an eye if he chose to.

Patti took a few more steps away.

He stared at her.

She let the air out of her lungs and forced a radiant Jamie smile even though she was more terrified than she'd ever been in her life. Perhaps, she should tell him she wasn't Jamie. Maybe he loved her sister enough to help Patti.

He might know who kidnapped Jamie.

She opened her mouth.

Or he might be the one who kidnapped her. She heard Jamie's voice telling her not to be an idiot. Not to be so naive and trusting.

She closed her mouth.

He gently caressed her face again. "You were supposed to be back days ago. I tried to reach you on your phone. I do not like it when I can't talk with you. I have been so worried."

This man didn't know what had happened to Jamie.

"I'm sorry. I didn't mean for you to worry, but it was unavoidable."

His hands slipped to her shoulders. Her stomach clenched, and she couldn't catch her breath. That bridge she hadn't wanted to cross moved closer and closer.

He stepped towards her, leaned down and kissed her with such passion it took her breath away.

Bile rose up in her throat. She pushed and stepped back from him.

His dark eyes flashed black with anger. "Is there a problem?"

She'd made a mistake, a big mistake, but there was

no way she could let this man touch her in such an intimate way.

Jamie, help me out. Tell me what to say, how to act.

Taking a deep breath, she turned toward him. "I'm not feeling well. I told you it was a rough trip, and I got home late. I'm exhausted. I'm sorry I didn't call but—"

His eyes were still angry, but his voice sounded calmer. "Yes, you should have. What happened with the merger?"

A merger.

Patti remembered Marcus telling her Jamie was a whiz at investing. That must be the cover Jamie used to leave often. She shook her head. "I don't want to talk about it now."

He gave her an odd look.

Jamie probably never said that in her life. It was hopeless. No way would Patti be able to convince this man she was Jamie. She still didn't know his name, but was sure he was the Mr. Hamed Robert had spoken of, and, no doubt, Jamie's lover.

But Patti couldn't call him Mr. Hamed.

Her stomach churned and her head throbbed. Why, oh, why hadn't she listened to Carter?

"Would you like some coffee?" she asked, trying to buy time.

"That would be fine," His voice was stilted and formal.

Patti felt her face flush with anxiety. Where did Jamie keep the coffee grinder? With the coffee, of course. She remembered seeing it last night as the delivery girl put away the groceries.

She opened the cupboard.

Thank You, God, thank you.

The grinder stood in its rightful spot beside the coffee beans. She pulled out the container, working hard to keep her hand from shaking. The only sound in the room was the whirring of the grinder.

The man walked up behind her and kissed her neck.

She forced herself not to flinch.

"You don't seem yourself, *ma cher.*"

No kidding.

She had to get away from this man. "How do you expect me to feel? It was a long trip and things went badly. First the merger problems, my cell phone, and then lost luggage and then—"

"Are you sure your luggage was lost? Perhaps it was confiscated."

"I don't know. I never thought of it, but why would my luggage be confiscated?"

"Who knows? Maybe the authorities are suspicious of you. The American government doesn't like Americans who keep close contact with my people."

She pretended to think and then turned back to him. "I doubt it. I'm sure it was plain old, bad luck. It happens, you know. Not everything—"

His black eyes pierced her like bullets. "Speaking of suspicions, my associates have voiced some suspicions of you."

25

Suspicions of you.

Her heart hammered and she felt as if she'd been sucker punched. How was she going to get out of this mess she'd created? She had to play along. And pray.

"Suspicious of me, why?"

"They question your loyalty to me and to our beliefs. They find it hard to trust an American for obvious reasons. They do not understand why you are always flying off to this place and that."

"But you understand, don't you?" she asked, making her voice lower.

He nodded as his finger trailed down her shoulder and along her arm. "I have tried to explain to them you have obligations because of your job. I have assured them you are loyal to me, and to them." His dark eyes pierced her own. "But now, the way you are acting today, I do not know. Perhaps..." His voice trailed off, his implication clear.

"I don't like the way that sounds," she said, suddenly angry, instead of terrified. She stared at him boldly.

Neither looked away, a battle of wills, which Jamie would win.

Patti didn't even breathe.

Can't back down.

He relented with a smile. "I know you are loyal, but now it is time for you to convince them."

Patti's heart raced, but she could breathe again. Did those words mean what she thought? If she could meet them, she might be able to find Jamie. "How am I supposed to do that?" With a theatrical sweep of her arms, she said, "I'm tired of all of this. Maybe we should forget abo—"

His black eyes turned darker. "I have obligations I must fulfill. Soon it will all be over and then we will leave."

It will all be over.

The words chilled her to the bone. What were these people planning?

Patti stared at the man who knew Jamie so well. Better than she did.

His skin was dark as if he worked outside or on a boat for a living. He wore an expensive tan linen suit which contrasted with his complexion. His black hair was long and wavy, giving him a rugged boyish look, though he appeared to be in his late thirties, or early forties.

She must get away from him before he discovered she wasn't Jamie.

If this man was Jamie's lover that probably meant he was a terrorist.

Terrorist.

Her throat dried up and she couldn't breathe. Why hadn't she listened to Carter? Too stubborn for her own good. And too selfish. She'd only been concerned about seeking absolution and assuaging her own guilt, rather than what was best for Sabrina.

God, I'm so sorry. I keep making stupid decisions.

It was imperative to convince this man she was Jamie until she could get away from him. "But what about me?" She whined as only Jamie could.

He threw up his hands. "I support you and take care of you. I bought you this beautiful apartment. Doesn't that show I love you?" He paced around the room. "I will quit the movement very soon, but the time is not right."

"I want to know what's going on."

He looked up in shock, obviously surprised she had the audacity to ask such a question.

Patti changed her tone and smiled. "I'm anxious for us to be together. How long before we can start our own life?"

"Not long," he promised her.

"Why will you not tell me? Don't you trust me?" Her heart threatened to jump out of her chest but she pressed on. Her sister might have died trying to find out what this man knew. "Tell me when this project you are working on will be done."

His black eyes darkened even more. "You know more than you should. If Rahmed knew the things I've told you, he would be very angry. I should never have let you become involved in any of this. It would have been better for you not to know."

Forgetting she was supposed to be Jamie, Patti jumped up. "But we will discuss it this time. You want me to give up everything for you. Then, you must show me you trust me. Tell me who this Rahmed is and what he is planning."

His face flushed and his eyes turned black with anger.

She'd gone too far.

The man walked toward her with a snarl on his face.

She shouldn't have pushed him.

But as he came closer to Patti, his face turned

almost gentle with only a hint of anger remaining. He touched her cheeks. "It has been so long since we have been together. Let's not fight, *ma cher*. We have better things to do with our time."

The bridge was right in front of her once again.

Her stomach clenched. She had to stop this, but she couldn't risk making him angry again. "I am too upset to think of such things. And now you tell me that Rahmed doesn't trust me. And you don't trust me enough to tell me what's happening. Instead you want to use me." Her voice took on an edge of hysteria she didn't have to fake.

"I have never used you. I love you." The steel in his eyes returned.

"I'm sorry. I didn't mean it like that." Tears began to flow. Real tears, considering her circumstances. "I told you I wasn't feeling well."

She looked away from him and her gaze landed on her purse. It occurred to her it contained her own ID not Jamie's. What an idiot she was. She walked over and grabbed it. She had to get out of this place now. Terrified, she started for the elevator.

She had to get to the elevator and out of this apartment, out of this town, and out of this state. The spacious room closed in on her.

An arm grabbed her elbow.

She turned toward this stranger—this terrorist.

"What are you doing? Where are you going?" He looked confused by the turn in the conversation. "I don't understand. Jamie, you seem different. You need to calm down."

"I am different. I...I..."

He patted her arm. "Is it that time of the month?"

Patti wanted to shout for joy. "Yes, yes, it is."

"Do not be upset. It is fine. I understand these things."

She smiled at him through her tears.

"Never be afraid to tell me the truth, Jamie. I love you, and I will never let anyone hurt you. I will protect you."

He might believe what he said, but Patti had a sinking feeling those words weren't true. Someone in his organization had gone behind his back.

"Have you forgotten? The Children's Fund Benefit is today." He looked at his watch. "And you are not ready."

"The Children's Fund Benefit is today?" She stammered out the words. For all she knew, Jamie could be in charge of the event. "I'd forgotten all about it. What time is it?"

"It's at noon." He gave her an odd look. "You need to get ready."

"I know. I know. Couldn't we skip it?" she asked, hoping to buy time.

He gave her a look of disdain.

"I'm sorry, of course, we can't miss it. I'm exhausted from the trip. I'm not thinking clearly. I still feel drained. Just give me time to take a shower and get dressed."

He still looked confused but he nodded, apparently satisfied with her answer. "I can make myself comfortable. I have calls to make, anyway."

She had to find a way to get him out of the apartment, so she could escape. Going into Jamie mode, Patti smiled coquettishly at him. "A woman needs private time to make herself beautiful for her man."

It was obvious her words pleased him.

His body language relaxed and he smiled at her. He pointed at his watch. "You do not have much time, but I will give you one hour."

"Fine," she managed to choke out. She would leave as soon as he left.

"I have a surprise for you. Rahmed will be at the benefit. You will finally meet him today." He touched her cheek and gave her a soft kiss before hitting the elevator button.

Patti stared at the closed elevator doors.

The man's words echoed.

Rahmed would be at this benefit. If she went, she would be able to meet Rahmed and learn his true identity.

Jamie had risked her life to meet this man.

If Patti had the courage, she could help Jamie before it was too late.

The only rational thing to do was to get on that elevator and leave, and then call Carter.

He was the professional.

The FBI could question the guests and discover who Rahmed was and then they could make him tell where Jamie was being held.

But maybe not.

They hadn't been able to discover who this monster was, even with Jamie being so involved in the situation.

Jamie's lover had freely used Rahmed's name several times as they talked.

Patti moved the puzzle pieces around and could only come up with one conclusion.

Whoever this Rahmed was, he had hidden his real identity so well they couldn't find him.

Patti expelled the breath she'd been holding. Patti

could finish the job for Jamie.

She would call Carter and tell him where she was and what was going on. He would help.

She grabbed her cell phone and flipped it open. The message icon flashed, but it was a number she didn't recognize. No time now to listen. Instead, she scrolled through calls until she found Carter's number. It was the same as the message number.

Carter had called her.

She heard the elevator moving. Who was it this time? Her purse was still in her hand. She slipped the phone in it, ignoring her racing heart.

The elevator thudded to a stop and her sister's lover walked out once again.

Her heart sank.

"You're back." She made the effort to sound welcoming. "I was afraid you were angry with me."

"I did not want to leave you alone when you are upset. You do not seem yourself today."

If he only knew.

She nodded, too terrified to move or speak.

"You haven't started getting ready yet, *ma cher*. The party starts soon. Today we cannot afford to be late."

"I don't know what to wear."

His eyes became guarded. "I thought that was what you bought the new outfit for. You look terrific in it."

She wasn't good at this spy stuff at all. In spite of her insides shaking worse than a senior waiting to hear if he passed his final exam, Patti gave him a bright sunny smile. "I know. I was having second thoughts about the dress, but you're right, it is the perfect thing to wear. I better go get ready. Make yourself comfortable, I'll try to hurry."

She turned and walked through the kitchen and back to Jamie's room, still clutching her purse. As she walked down the hall, she passed a door she hadn't checked the previous night.

It was locked, but when she twisted the lock popped up. She opened the door, hoping the man in the living room wouldn't hear.

More doors. One was marked stairs.

Her muscles relaxed as she read the words. It was her way out. All she had to do was close the door behind her and leave. She could be far from this building before Jamie's lover knew she'd even left.

Patti stood between the two doors staring back and forth.

One door led to freedom and her safety.

The other door led back to a terrorist.

26

Carter unbuckled his seatbelt and stood. He needed to convince someone to let him off the plane. His cell phone wasn't working and he had to get to a land line. Every minute he was stuck here became more dangerous for Patti.

He walked down the aisle to an attendant. He spoke in a calm tone. "I know you're really busy and things are hectic, but can I talk to you for a minute?" He ended the request with his best smile.

She eyed him with suspicion, but smiled back. "Do you have a problem, sir?"

"Actually, I do." He pulled his badge out of his hip pocket and showed it to her. "I'm a police officer, and I'm working on an extremely dangerous case. I need to be somewhere else."

"I know. I know. Everybody needs to be somewhere else. I get it." Frustration edged into the attendant's voice. "I'm doing everything I can. We're going to be cleared for take-off soon, sir."

"I understand, but if I could get off the plane. I could call some other people who could help this woman. She's in serious trouble."

"You can use your cell phone." The flight attendant pointed out.

"My phone's not working. I asked a couple other people but theirs aren't working, either."

"Oh, I'm sorry." The woman looked past Carter, keeping a close eye on the other passengers. She turned back to Carter. "Nothing I can do about that."

"I've got to get out of here. It's an emergency."

The flight attendant listened with a sweet smile pasted on her face, and then said, "I'm really very sorry, but it's not possible. Federal regulations won't permit it."

"But—"

A man dressed in a jogging suit stepped up behind the attendant. "Is there a problem, Marcy?"

The air marshal, no doubt. He looked capable enough.

"No problem." Marcy gave him a meaningful look.

Carter stepped towards the man, showing him his badge. "Are you the air marshal?"

The man nodded.

Carter went through his spiel again, but with the same results.

Frustrated, Carter marched back to his seat and looked at his phone. No signal.

Lord, protect her.

27

San Francisco, California

Patti stood between the two doors, searching for an answer. A spark of anger ignited inside her.

These terrorists wanted to kill Americans.

Jamie didn't want that to happen. Her sister may have given the ultimate to prevent it. In spite of the danger to herself, Jamie had worked hard to meet this Rahmed. Jamie was fearless and relentless. If Jamie hadn't wimped out, then neither would she.

The spark kindled a fire of determination she didn't know she had. How dare these people hurt her sister? How dare these people want to hurt her country? Patti choked back a sob. She wasn't going to let them get away with it.

She would go to the party and she would meet Rahmed. Once she learned his alias, she would slip away and find the nearest police station. It was a simple plan, but it would work. She would finish what Jamie started.

One last glance at the exit sign and she stepped back into the apartment. She went to the adjoining bathroom and locked the door. She turned on the shower to muffle what she was doing. Slipping her phone out, she listened to Carter's messages.

She hit the send button to call Carter. He'd be able to contact Marcus and the FBI to help her. The phone rang, but in the next moment her sister's lover called to her from the other side of the door. "Jamie?"

"I'm in the shower." She called back and slipped the phone back in her purse. Taking off her clothes, she jumped into the shower. She let the hot water pour over her.

Things like this didn't happen to people like her. Feeling overwhelmed, she prayed. A sense of peace descended over her.

Patti would finish this. If she could, she thought with trepidation. She shook her head. No negative thoughts.

She stepped out of the shower, dried her hair, and wrapped herself in a towel. Taking a deep breath, she opened the bathroom door. He sat on the bed waiting for her. Her heart thudded. She couldn't let him see her naked. Jamie had a birthmark, she didn't. He might not notice, but she couldn't take the chance.

"That was just what the doctor ordered. I feel much better." She pointed at him and giggled. "And you need to go. The next time you see me, I will be beeeutiful. Now, out-out-out."

"You are always beautiful, *ma cher*."

She batted her eyelashes. "So sweet of you to say. In that case, I guess I'm going to be stupendous." Putting a hand on her hip, she tilted her head.

"OK, OK. I'm leaving." He laughed.

When he shut the door, she sank to the bed. Her knees shook. Taking a deep breath, she stood. No time to relax.

Jamie's closet was the size of a small room. Unlike the one back in Florida, this closet was filled with clothes of every sort. Casual, dress, or sporty and shoes to match.

A testament to the differences in her sister's two lifestyles.

She searched through the clothes until she found an outfit with the tags still on. It better be the right one, or Mr. Hamed might think she'd lost her mind—again.

It was a simple a-line dress but the silkiness of the blue flowered material flowed over her curves, giving an elegance that belied the casual style. The soft halter top fit like a second skin and exposed more cleavage than Patti had ever shown.

The dress fell to the mid calf area of her leg but made up for the modesty with a slit up the side. She went back to the closet and found a pair of matching blue stilettos. She stood in front of the mirror and looked at herself.

She blinked with amazement. Gone was the school marm. Instead, an elegant partygoer stared back. Clothes did make the person. Stumbling, she walked back in the bathroom. No way could she wear those stilettos. She'd make a fool of herself.

Searching the closet once again, she found a pair of white sandals-no heels. Not the pizzazz of the stilettos but she could walk in them. They would have to do.

As she rooted through the make-up drawer in the bathroom, she gasped. A small gun lay at the back of the drawer. Her stomach turned. Why did her sister need a gun?

After she'd put on make-up, she fluffed her new hairstyle with her fingers and looked in the mirror. The transformation was complete. She no longer looked or felt like Patti, the school teacher, but like Jamie, a woman who lived on the edge. She hoped she could keep up the facade well enough to not get herself killed.

She opened up the make-up drawer once again. She hated guns. Closing her eyes, she took a deep breath and picked it up. Stuffing it in her purse, she prayed she wouldn't have to use it.

Footsteps warned her he was on his way back to the bedroom.

He opened the door without knocking. His eyes widened in appreciation. As she stood there, feeling vulnerable, he came to her. His huge arms enfolded her. "You look beautiful." His voice trembled.

She didn't understand.

He seemed to love Jamie.

She took a step back and smiled up at him. "How am I supposed to meet Rahmed at the party?"

"It is simple. We will go to the party, and you will be introduced to Rahmed. You must act respectful of him at all times. Rahmed is traditional and believes women should always be respectful of men."

"How will I know it's him?" If she could get him to tell her Rahmed's current alias, there would be no need to go to the party.

"You will know him. I have no doubt about that."

"Maybe, you should tell me his name, now. I want to make sure I don't act disrespectful in any way."

"No reason to know now. You will meet him soon enough. He may want to talk to you in private for a few moments. That will be your opportunity to convince him you are loyal to the movement."

"Will it be dangerous?"

"Not if you convince him of your true feelings."

That was the problem, wasn't it?

She wasn't the born actress Jamie was.

Patti prayed. She didn't know how, but God would give her the words she needed.

He brushed her hair away from her face. "You will do fine. Just be yourself. He will love you as I do." He waited a moment and looked at her. "After all, Rahmed is my brother."

"Your brother?" Her shock as the words sank in was real.

He nodded. His face was solemn. "Yes, I tell you this because I want you to know I do trust you. I trust you with all my secrets."

Patti put her head down, and then looked back up at him. "Thank you."

He patted her shoulder. "Soon, none of this will matter to us. This is my last assignment and Rahmed knows this. The movement will continue without me. I am one small piece. It will not stop our ultimate goal." His eyes glowed with fanaticism. "We will succeed."

She forced a smile, but his words chilled her heart and soul.

છેઙ

As they rode down the elevator, Patti was too terrified to speak for fear of saying the wrong thing. She had a feeling the man with her didn't speak unless he had something to say.

"How do you feel?"

"Terrified."

He squeezed her hand. "Do not be afraid. I will take care of you."

As long as he thought she was Jamie, he would do what he could to keep her safe.

As the elevator door slid open, Robert stood at the reception desk deep in conversation with the grocery delivery girl.

They both looked up and stared at her.

Even from across the room, she saw the confusion written on their faces.

Patti felt her face flush.

It was as if they knew she wasn't Jamie.

She dismissed the idea as her overactive paranoia.

Robert turned back and said something to the delivery girl.

She nodded, but continued to stare at Patti.

Robert marched in their direction with a look of determination on his face.

Her heart sank.

If Robert voiced his suspicions in front of this man, it would ruin everything.

"Ms. Jakowski, I need to talk to you for a minute."

She shook her head and begged him with her eyes to go away.

"We have no time. We are in a hurry." Her companion snapped in an impatient tone.

Robert smiled amiably at the man, ignoring his tone. "Nice to see you again, Mr. Hamed. I'm sorry, but this will only take a minute. Miss Jakowski forgot to sign the grocery slip from last night again. She does it all the time. Carrie will be in big trouble at the store if she doesn't get the signature right now."

Patti remembered signing. "No, I'm sure—"

Something in Robert's gaze stopped her from saying more.

"We don't want Carrie to lose her job. It'll only take a minute, Miss Jakowski. I promise."

"Of course, it's not a problem." Patti gave a little shrug and smile. She patted Mr. Hamed's arm. "Don't worry. I'll take care of this and be right back. It won't take but a moment."

Patti's heart pounded as she walked over to Carrie at the reception counter. She wiped her sweaty palms on the dress, hoping it didn't stain.

Carrie's eyes were filled with concern as she whispered with urgency, "Jamie, are you OK? Are you in some kind of trouble?"

Patti fought the urge to scream no, I'm not OK. "Of course I'm fine, Carrie. Where's the grocery slip?"

Carrie handed her the slip from the night before.

In an instant, Patti understood the confusion and concern. In big letters, Patti looked at her own name, Patti Jakowski. She was really bad at this spy stuff.

"Oh, I see." Patti looked at Carrie, tired of the deception. Making a decision, she took a deep breath and glanced back at Robert and Jamie's lover. She whispered, "Look, I don't have time to explain. Trust me, this is very import—"

"But—" The girl handed her a new grocery slip and a pen.

She gave Carrie a comforting pat. "Thanks for being worried. But I have a question for you. It's going to sound strange, but please, I don't have time to answer your questions."

Patti turned her back so her unknown companion couldn't see her face. She didn't want him to get suspicious.

He was already scowling in their direction, ignoring Robert's attempts at conversation.

"Is the man I'm with Mr. Hamed?"

Carrie nodded, even though she must have been totally confused. "Yes, of course. You know—"

"Do you know his first name?"

Carrie's mouth fell open in shock. "I've heard you call him Joseph. Jamie, what's going—"

"Thanks, I'll explain later."

Patti rushed back to Robert and Joseph Hamed. She refrained from doing a happy dance. "All ready, Joseph. Let's go have some fun."

He nodded with a terse expression, but didn't react to the name so Carrie must have been right.

Robert held the door open for them.

Patti squinted as she walked out in the bright afternoon sunshine, surprised to see a conspicuous white limo waiting. She turned to Joseph Hamed. "Is that for us?"

Joseph appeared pleased she was impressed. "I saw no reason for us not to go in style. Everyone else will be."

She had no idea terrorists lived in such luxury. She tossed her hair as Jamie would. Instead of going to a party, she felt as if she were going to an execution. Her own. "Absolutely."

The driver of the limo stood at attention, holding the car door open for them. The man practically bowed to Joseph as they walked up to the car.

Looking back, Patti waved at Robert.

"Have a good day." Robert said, waving them off. "You both look like you're dressed to have some fun."

Joseph Hamed smiled briefly at Robert. "We are going to the yacht party for the Children's Fund Benefit."

Robert nodded and gave a deprecating smile. "Don't let me keep you, then. Have a wonderful time."

Robert turned and walked back to Carrie, who stood at the door still holding the sales receipt in her hand.

Worry marred Carrie's pretty face.

Joseph nodded at the driver. "How is your family,

Rakeem? I pray they are fine."

"They are, sir. I can't thank you enough for helping to get them visas to enter this country. If ever I can do something for you..." The driver's voice trailed off.

Joseph Hamed held up a hand. "It was nothing. I was glad to do it. We will not speak of it again. You owe me nothing. We are friends, and friends do favors for each other from time to time, but you owe me nothing." His last words were spoken slower and with more stress.

Rakeem nodded, gratitude shining in his gaze as he looked at Joseph Hamed. Almost hero worship.

Patti slid into the seat and Joseph shut the door.

The two men walked to the other side.

The driver held the door for Joseph while he climbed into the limo.

Patti glanced back to find Robert and Carrie still staring.

Both faces mirrored the concern Patti felt.

Patti sat in the luxurious limo thinking about the words exchanged between Joseph and the driver. The dots connected and understanding dawned. It all made so much sense when she thought about it.

Joseph Hamed helped his countrymen to get to the land of opportunity legally and then one day, Rakeem and the others would be asked to do some small favor for Joseph and his friends.

Perhaps, to deliver a package, or let a stranger stay at his house for a few days. Whatever it was, it would seem harmless.

This sincere new American would probably never know he betrayed his new homeland.

An appalling thought.

Patti balled her hands into fists. In a country as large and as free as the United States, there could be thousands of innocent people like Rakeem being manipulated into helping with terrorist acts and not even be aware of it.

Only the inner circle knew the master plan, the ultimate goal.

She shuddered.

"Are you cold, *ma cher*?" She shook her head, but he put a hand to her forehead to check her temperature.

She struggled not to slap it away.

"You may indeed have caught something on your trip. Airplanes are notorious germ carriers."

She nodded, but didn't trust herself to speak.

Sirens blared from behind them.

A police car was following with lights on.

Had Carter figured out where she was and they were about to pull her out of the limo and ruin her chance to find her sister's kidnapper?

Patti decided she was seeing this deception through to the end. She wouldn't let these people blow her cover if she could help it.

Rakeem slowed and pulled to the curb.

Joseph muttered words in his native tongue under his breath, but turned to smile at her. "It is fine, I am sure. Rakeem is a good driver and he did not break any traffic laws. Just a minor inconvenience."

Perhaps Carrie and Robert called the police. Told them some crazy woman was pretending to be Jamie.

Or the FBI had shown up and Robert told them the type of vehicle she'd left in.

Or maybe Carter or Marcus...there could be a thousand different things going on instead of a routine traffic stop.

She held her breath.

If the policeman tried to make her leave, she would refuse.

The cop walked up and bent down to stare at the window dividing them from the driver. The officer motioned at the window.

He was looking for her. She just knew it. Patti prepared for whatever was about to happen. She hoped he wouldn't ask for an ID. Hers said Patti Jakowski, not Jamie.

Joseph pressed a button and the window slid down.

"Good afternoon, Officer. Is there a problem?" Joseph asked.

The officer stared at Joseph, then at Patti. "Not that I know of." He turned back to Rakeem. "I need to see your chauffeur's license and the city operating permit."

Rakeem handed them to the officer as requested.

The officer took them and walked away without comment.

Joseph whispered to Patti. "This is the kind of harassment we are exposed to in this country."

Patti bit her tongue but wanted to scream. She nodded with what she hoped was a concerned look on her face, but her mind raced with worry.

"Just ridiculous." Joseph muttered.

The officer returned. He bent down and peered into the back seat.

It took every ounce of strength not to look away from him. She was sure she'd look suspicious if she did.

"Officer, we are in a hurry. We are on our way to a children's benefit. We must arrive before—"

The young officer held up a hand and turned back to the limo driver. "Could you come with me, please?"

Anger seethed from Joseph.

Rakeem opened his door and walked to the back of the limo.

Patti fought the urge to twist around to see what was happening.

Patti and Joseph waited in silence.

Rakeem returned in less than ten minutes.

Joseph waited for them to drive away before he spoke.

"What was the problem?"

"J...just a broken tail light, sir." Rakeem stammered. "Nothing to worry about."

Patti breathed a sigh of relief.

"Did he ask you any questions?" Joseph's tone changed from kind benefactor to interrogator.

"N...not really. Just made conversation, asked me questions. How I liked this country and why I came. He wanted to know how I got my visa."

"And what did you tell him?"

"I told him I loved America. It is a great country."

Joseph shook his head. "No, no. What did you tell him regarding your visa?"

"I told them I won it in a lottery held in my country once every year."

"Good, good. Did they ask about me?"

"No."

Joseph nodded his approval at Rakeem. "Very good, very good."

Joseph hit the button and the glass slid up. Joseph turned his focus back to Patti. He picked up her hand and placed it to his lips. "You are trembling, *ma cher*. Are you all right?"

"A little nervous."

"But it is what you have wanted for so long. Rahmed is my brother. No need to worry. He will love you as I do."

"I know, but..." Patti's voice trailed off.

This man seemed so confident that he could keep her safe and yet Jamie was missing.

Could she be on the wrong track? Perhaps Jamie's disappearance had nothing to do with these people.

"He will meet you and everything will be settled. Then, I will complete my final assignment."

Settled.

Perhaps, but not in the way Joseph expected.

If she had her way, Joseph and his brother would be in custody before the end of the night and Jamie would be home. If she didn't have her way...well...Patti shuddered at the thought.

He patted her hand. He reached for her and pulled her close to him. "I haven't seen you for such a long time."

She allowed his arms to stay around her, though she was repulsed. She couldn't risk his anger again. She changed the subject. "I know, Joseph. You are a good man." She allowed herself to lean against him and hoped she sounded more loving than she felt. "It hasn't been easy for you."

"You helped me to become a better person, Jamie."

The more time she spent with Joseph the more she believed he did love Jamie.

Could Jamie have truly been planning a life with him?

She squeezed his hand. "And you have done the same for me."

"We will go to the party. Rahmed will meet you

and see you are trustworthy. He will love you as I do. Stop worrying and have a good time. It will be a wonderful party."

She turned and smiled at him, praying she'd still be alive at the end of the party.

28

Their limo slowed due to a long line of limos waiting to drop off the other partygoers.

Jumbled thoughts raced through Patti's mind. How was she ever going to pull off this charade?

She had no idea if Jamie's friends would be there. She could walk right past them without knowing it. Did Jamie know the host and hostess of the benefit? Would she be able to fool them? Her mind jumped from question to question.

And with each new question her heart raced faster. She thought she might pass out, or have a heart attack before they even arrived at the yacht.

Joseph laid a hand on her arm.

She forced a smile when she looked at him.

"You will like Kathryn and H.H. They do a lot of good with their money. They have donated their time, money, and yacht for this benefit."

Relief flooded through her. One question answered. Perhaps, she could find out more information for the FBI. "Are they involved with you know…your other activities? Do they help fund those activities, too?"

Joseph's hand rested lightly on her arm but as she spoke, it tightened into an iron grip.

Another mistake.

She needed to keep her mouth shut, or she'd never

make it to the party.

His voice was low with irritation. "Why would you ask such a question? You know H.H. and I have been business associates only. You know this."

Too late to do anything but bluff her way out of the situation. Patti shrugged. "Sorry. Of course. I was trying to make conversation." She smiled at him in apology.

He didn't smile back. Instead his eyes assessed her in a cold, clinical way. "I do not like when you talk of such things."

In a twinkling, she knew without a doubt what Jamie would do. She flung her head back with a careless attitude and gave a deep, throaty laugh. "But I'm an American woman and we're not passive little wallflowers who sit around and look pretty. That's not who I am. If you want someone like that..." She moved away from him.

It worked.

The hand on her arm relaxed. "I know. I know. But you must learn to control what you say. Your tongue could get you in trouble, especially with Rahmed. Let's not fight."

"Let's not." She scooted closer to him, trying to forget that the man made her skin crawl. She willed her body to not tremble. Patti felt beads of sweat pop out on her hands.

Only three cars before their turn.

Hopefully, she would meet this Rahmed soon, learn his name, and get off the yacht so she could contact Carter.

Her heart lurched at the thought of Carter. It had been a mistake to run off and leave him. He could be here helping her had she not been so quick to judge his motives. People didn't always have to conform to her way of thinking. If she'd learned that sooner, she and Jamie might be sitting on Jamie's veranda enjoying the Florida sun. Instead, she was about to come face to face with a monster.

Staring at the yacht, she wondered how she'd get through this.

"I had no idea," she mumbled. She looked back at him. "Wow! It's amazing."

Joseph nodded. "Her family dates back to the beginning of the oil business in this country. The yacht belongs to her family. H.H., of course, has his own money, but nothing like Kathryn."

As they waited to disembark from the limo, Joseph picked up her hand.

Patti fought the urge to pull away.

The car moved up and it was their turn.

Rakeem opened Joseph's door and then Joseph walked around the limo to open her car door.

If things went her way, she'd meet Rahmed soon and then she could leave this whole nightmare behind. She took a deep breath and stepped out.

He very gallantly offered his arm to Patti, and they walked up the gangplank of the enormous yacht.

Patti imagined herself as Jamie, the actress, and held her head high. She walked languidly up the red carpeted gangplank as if she didn't have a care in the world, knowing at any minute she'd meet a terrorist.

Once on board, she saw a receiving line. More butterflies.

Did Jamie know any of these people?

Her stomach churned.

With a gentle touch, Joseph guided her towards the line, his voice solicitous. "Come, I will introduce you to our hosts."

"Why don't we wait until later? When the line is shorter."

He scowled and shook his head. "It is important we follow protocol."

"Of course, it was just a suggestion." Patti thought she might be sick. In the best of times, she wasn't the most socially graceful person.

Act like Jamie. Act like Jamie.

Joseph pointed out a woman as they waited for their turn. "The woman in blue is Kathryn Hart."

"Pretty." She was beautiful, but not flashy. Her long brown hair blew in the wind. She had on a mid-calf length turquoise dress that was sleek and accented her curves, but the summer print made her appear ready to take a walk on the beach, not host a party on a yacht for hundreds of the rich and famous.

When it was their turn, Joseph guided her forward with his hand firmly on her elbow, as if he thought she might bolt.

It seemed like a good idea to her.

"Kathryn, this is Jamie Jakowski."

Kathryn grabbed Patti's hand as if they'd known each other for years. "Jamie, it is wonderful to finally meet you. Joseph's told me all about you. He's been like a different man since he met you. You've made him very happy."

"Just as he's made me very happy." Smiling, Patti tried to match her hostess's gracious manner. "It's nice to meet you. Everything looks simply fabulous."

The man standing beside Kathryn looked over and smiled. He was tall and older than Kathryn. "Not as fabulous as you." He held out a hand. "I'm Harold Hart the third, but everyone calls me H.H."

"Well then, I guess I'll call you Harry." Patti tilted her head and winked. The group laughed. "I like to be different."

H.H. turned to the man and woman standing beside them and made more introductions. "This is Raymond and Maria Hammond. Maria is the co-chair of the event and has been so helpful with all of this. She was indispensable to Kathryn and myself. We couldn't have pulled it off without her. Raymond is a fellow financier, much like yourself."

As H.H. spoke, Joseph squeezed her hand, hard enough to make her glance at him. *Raymond Hammond. Rahmed Hamed.* It made sense. This had to be the man Jamie wanted to meet so desperately.

Patti wanted to cheer. Time to leave, now that she'd learned his alias.

Raymond's gaze met hers. His black eyes blazed and his mouth twisted in rage.

Her heart stopped beating. *He knows I'm not Jamie...*Patti trembled, not wanting to think about what it meant. If she fell apart now, it would ruin her plan.

In an instant, Raymond replaced his sneer with a gracious smile, but his eyes were cold as he stared at her. He reached for her hand, but she was frozen, not able to move.

Joseph nudged her arm forward.

Every part of her wanted to scream—*terrorist*. In her mind, she saw herself announcing to the others that the man was a terrorist. But in the next second, she saw Raymond and Joseph laughing and telling the others she must be having a mental breakdown, and they would take her to the hospital.

No one would ever hear from her again.

Not a good idea, she decided.

"It's nice to meet you, Jamie." His mouth twisted into a sneer as he said the name. He grasped her hand, but instead of shaking it, he moved it to his lips and gave it a gentle kiss. His eyes mocked her.

Patti wanted to slap the man.

"And this is my wife, Maria. The two of you must make time to talk later. I'm sure you will both find it very enlightening."

What kind of a woman married a terrorist?

Pulling her hand away from his, she turned to his wife.

Maria Hammond didn't look well. Her eyes were puffy and bloodshot. She looked as if she hadn't slept in days.

Patti looked back at Raymond, taking him up on his challenge. "Sounds like a great idea. Maria, are you a native-born...Californian?"

"Not at all. I grew up in Pennsylvania."

As Patti shook her hand, Maria's fingers trembled. "Then, I guess we were practically neighbors growing up, since I'm from Ohio."

"Ohio?" Joseph sounded confused. "I thought you were from New York."

Raymond laughed. "Oh, I'm sure Jamie has a few more secrets that you know nothing about, Joseph. American women are like that. Are they not, Jamie?" His tone was soft enough others around them would not hear. Raymond leaned forward. "Please stay in this area. I will need to talk with both of you. We have urgent business to take care of." His words were a command, not a request.

I'm the urgent business he's talking about.

She had to get off this ship.

Joseph nodded. "Of course, Raymond, Jamie and I

will be waiting for you."

Looking at them, Patti saw a family resemblance and wondered if anyone else noticed it.

Joseph appeared to be the older, but there was no mistaking who was dominant—Raymond.

They walked away from the receiving line and wandered among the other partygoers on the deck.

Her mind raced, trying to figure out how to get away.

Raymond Hammond.

"We need to stay close by. Remember, Raymond wants to talk with us."

He doesn't want to talk with me. He wants to kill me.

She grabbed Joseph's arm and urged him forward. "He'll be able to find us, but let's look around. No reason not to have fun while we wait."

Joseph planted his feet and the stubborn look on his face told her it wasn't going to be that easy.

She leaned close and whispered in his ear. "Come on, Joseph. We won't go far, but it's a shame to miss a great party."

He relented. "I suppose."

Servers in brightly colored Hawaiian shirts with white shorts and real leis around their necks wove their way through the crowd, offering drinks and appetizers. Long black wigs adorning the female servers made them look even more exotic.

A waitress stopped in front of Joseph and Patti. "Sir, what would you like? These Bahama Mamas are tasty, but I can bring you something stronger if you wish."

Joseph looked at Patti. "What would you like, Jamie?"

The last thing Patti needed was alcohol, but she

was supposed to be having a good time. She smiled at Joseph. "Bahama Mama sounds great to me."

His eyes widened, but he said nothing.

Too late to make a different choice.

She picked up two glasses and handed one to Joseph. She held hers up and clinked Joseph's glass.

He tapped his glass against hers, but didn't smile.

29

An old Springsteen song blared as they strolled along the deck.

Several well-known actors and one of her favorite writers were among the partygoers, not that she cared.

Her mind was focused on only one thing. Finding a way off the yacht.

Her attempts to leave had been unsuccessful so far.

Joseph was sticking to her like glue.

If she tried to leave again, he'd become suspicious.

Joseph looked at his watch. "We need to find Raymond."

In spite of the heat of the sunny day, a chill crept down her spine.

This was it.

"You're right. You go find Raymond while I find the powder room, and then I'll be right back."

Joseph tightened his grip on her arm. "What is wrong with you? For months, all you wanted to do was meet Rahmed and now you act as if you're trying to avoid him. Rahmed wants to speak to both of us."

"And he will, as soon as I find a bathroom." Her voice was firm, but her insides were quivering. Her gaze roved over the sea of people. If she could just mix in with the crowd of people, she could disappear. She attempted to move out of his grasp, but he held on firmly.

Joseph spotted a group of two men and one woman who were standing apart from the crowd. He waved a hand and caught their attention. The group moved towards them. "There is Dennis with Suzanne. She can help you find the restroom."

Patti protested. "I'm quite capable of finding it myself."

"Suzanne is your friend. You do not want to see her?" Joseph spoke in such a sharp tone, Patti had no choice.

She'd find a way to ditch the woman as soon as they were out of Joseph's sight.

Joseph leaned close to the one man and said something.

In turn, Suzanne's escort whispered something in Suzanne's ear.

Joseph looked at Patti. "Suzanne will help you find the powder room."

Joseph was becoming more suspicious by the moment.

The men walked away, leaving Patti and Suzanne alone.

"Jamie, Jamie." Suzanne sounded breathless. "Isn't this divine? Have you ever seen such extravagance? Isn't it marvelous?" She laughed and Patti joined in, not understanding what she was laughing about.

Suzanne was short, even shorter than Patti's five feet, four inches. But shortness didn't stop Suzanne from being elegant. She wore a white full-length dress which complemented her deep tan. The dress itself was strapless with a bodice that sparkled more than snow on a moonlit night. She showed enough cleavage to be more than a little noticeable.

"Great dress," Patti commented.

Suzanne cocked her head and stared at Patti. "You were there when I bought it."

Oops.

"I know. I meant it looks wonderful on you."

The woman twirled.

Patti noticed Suzanne's heels were at least three inches high.

Patti looked around, trying to figure out how to get off the yacht.

"What's wrong?" Suzanne asked.

"Nothing. I need to powder my nose. That's all."

Suzanne grabbed her arm, her voice desperate. "Come on. Let's get some food. I haven't eaten for a week."

Looking at Suzanne, Patti could believe she was telling the truth.

"Where's Dennis and Joseph?" Patti asked.

They walked into a ballroom. Music blared. The band played another Springsteen tune. She looked closer at the band and her mouth fell open. *Never mind. Focus on getting off the yacht, not the man entertaining.*

The crowd sang and a few brave people were dancing.

Others stood in small groups talking, and still others were sitting at tables.

At one side of the room were large buffet tables laden with food.

"Let's eat," said Suzanne. She grabbed Patti's elbow and led her towards the food tables.

Patti pulled away from Suzanne. "I'm not hungry. You go get food and I'll find us a table. But first, I need to find a bathroom."

"No." It came out sounding like an order. There was a desperate glint in Suzanne's eyes.

Patti stopped and looked at her "Why not?"

Suzanne looked sheepish and shrugged. "No reason. I didn't want to go to the buffet by myself."

"Let's go get a table first." Once they found a seat, Patti took another sip of her drink.

Suzanne stopped talking and gawked at her. Patti's stomach churned. Looking at Suzanne's face left no doubt she'd make a mistake. "What's wrong?"

"What are you drinking, Jamie?"

"Bahama Mama. It tastes great."

Suzanne stared at Patti for a moment.

Her demeanor changed and a look of puzzlement graced her face. Her voice echoed the same confusion. "But I thought you were an alcoholic. I've never seen you drink before."

Patti looked at Suzanne and then at the drink.

Her heart sank as she remembered when Joseph handed her the drink.

He hadn't just given her a drink. He'd given her a test and she'd failed.

❧

Carter hiked through the San Francisco terminal, making plans for how to find Marcus, and then Patti. He'd take a taxi to the local FBI office first. He didn't care how irritated the people in that office became, they would locate Marcus for him, or pay the consequences.

He pulled out his cell phone. Hopefully, the reception would be better now that he was on the ground. He hit the redial button hoping Patti would pick up this time. No such luck. It went straight to voice mail. Her phone must be turned off.

"Carter." A voice yelled.

He turned.

Marcus marched towards him.

Breathing a sigh of relief, Carter wasted no time getting to him. Obviously, his call to the FBI office produced results. Marcus must've checked the airlines to find his flight number and meet up with him.

"Thank God, you're here, we've got big problems. Patti is in San Francisco somewhere. She flew out here last night."

"What?" Marcus yelled. "She's going to get herself killed."

"I've been calling her cell, but no answer. It must be turned off. She found Jamie's address."

"Got any luggage?"

Carter shook his head.

"Let's go. I'll fill you in while we drive. I'm right out front. One of the few FBI privileges."

Carter and Marcus walked through the sliding glass door with a dozen other people.

A car sat at the curb. A blue Honda Civic that had seen better days. He glanced over at Marcus with an arched eyebrow. "I guess the FBI doesn't pay well."

"Shut up. I borrowed it from an agent. They're supposed to be getting me a rental car, but they keep having an excuse why they haven't done it. Budget cuts, you know. We've had no luck finding Jamie. Her apartment and office have been checked. A few friends have been contacted, but not many. We didn't want to alert the wrong people. We've been looking for her companion, but can't seem to find him, either."

"What's his name?"

Marcus looked both ways and then turned right on red. "His name is Joseph Hamed. We haven't been able to find a paper trail linking him to any known terrorist activity, but according to what he tells Jamie the link is there. He won't give her any specific details and we can't find any evidence to arrest or convict the man."

"How long has Jamie been working on this case?"

"Not quite a year. She knew Hamed socially and when she reestablished contact with him, she overheard something that made her suspicious. We started investigating, and she got more involved than she should have." Marcus took his gaze off the road and looked at Carter. "Hamed is Sabrina's father."

What a mess for Sabrina. Her mother was most likely dead, and her father was a suspected terrorist. And her aunt was missing.

"We've got to find Patti, or that little girl ends up alone."

"Not true. My wife and I will gladly make her part of our family."

That eased his mind for Sabrina, but not for Patti.

"Jamie had no idea he was a terrorist. She looked him up to tell him about Sabrina. That's when she came to me. I should have told her to ignore it and disappear from the man's life. Thank goodness, she never told him about Sabrina."

"So Hamed is in charge of the cell?"

"A man known by the name of Rahmed is. We haven't got a clue who Rahmed really is. That was Jamie's assignment. To identify the name this man operates under."

"Apparently, she got too close to finding the truth."

"That's the way it looks."

Marcus pulled up in front of an apartment

building. He hadn't shut off the motor before a short, balding man rushed over to them.

"Sorry sir, you can't park in front of the building. This is a no parking zone."

Ignoring the request, they both stepped out of the car.

The doorman pointed at the car and raised his voice a few notches. "Didn't you hear me? This is a no parking zone, sir. You can't park here. You have to move this car." The word car was said with particular distaste. "Immediately."

Marcus flashed his FBI badge at the man, and then slipped it back in his pocket. The man didn't seem impressed.

"Can I see your badge a bit longer, officer?" He sniffed as though the word smelled bad.

"Sure. No problem," responded Marcus with an easy smile. He pulled the badge back out andgave it to the doorman. The doorman examined it for several long moments before he handed it to Marcus.

"Well, I guess if anyone can park here, you can," the doorman said with a wry grin. He stuck his hand out to Marcus and then to Carter. "I wasn't trying to hassle you, just doing my job. No hard feelings."

"No problem."

"Can I help you with something, sir?" the doorman asked.

Carter made a motion of deference to Marcus. After all, it was the FBI's investigation.

Marcus gazed back at the doorman. "I'm Special Agent Marcus Hanks. "

"I'm Robert McDonald."

Carter bit his tongue as they exchanged pleasantries.

"Well, Robert, I need to know the last time you saw Jamie Jakowski."

A puzzled expression crossed Robert's face. "Why do you want to know?"

"If you don't mind I'll ask the questions," Marcus's tone was calm, but firm.

Robert's bald head shone in the brightness of the afternoon. "I can't give out information about our tenants. Is she in some sort of trouble?"

Marcus stepped closer to the man. "Why do you ask?"

Robert shrugged and took several steps away from Marcus. "It's the second time the FBI has been here about Ms. Jakowski. They asked me to call when she got home, but she said it was all straightened out. She's a lovely person and I wouldn't want her to be in any trouble."

"That's what we're trying to find out, Robert. We want to know if she's in any trouble, as well," Carter broke in before Marcus could say more. "Again, when was the last time you saw Ms. Jakowski?"

Robert glanced up to the sky, then back at Marcus. "I guess I would have to say today."

"You don't sound very positive." Before the doorman could respond, Marcus asked another question. "And when did she get home from her business trip?"

"I can't..."

"Yes, Robert, you can tell me, and I suggest you do, or I can take you down to the FBI offices and we can continue this conversation there." His demeanor had changed from an easygoing good guy to cop, in the blink of an eye.

Robert stammered his response. "L...l...ast night."

"Has she been acting differently?"

Carter didn't miss the surprise on the doorman's face. He watched the internal struggle play out on Robert's face and lost his patience. He took a menacing step towards the doorman. "Look, we aren't playing games. We need your help."

Fear danced across Robert's face as he stepped back. "I'm not trying to play games, really. It's just I'm not sure. Something strange did happen and well...I'm not sure."

"What happened?" Marcus and Carter both asked at the same time.

"Ms. Jakowski came home last night, or at least, I thought it was her, but she's been acting strangely. Not quite herself." He squirmed.

"How so?" Carter asked.

"It's sorta crazy. First she told me she lost her key along with her luggage."

"So? That makes sense," Carter said.

"We don't use keys. We have the magnetic cards, sir. Then Carrie, the girl who delivers groceries, came over last night like she always does when Jamie returns from a trip. When she came back down, she said Jamie was acting pretty weird."

"OK, maybe she was tired," Marcus suggested.

"Nah, Carrie came by today and showed me the grocery receipt Jamie signed. She signed the receipt with the wrong first name, and then when Carrie –"

"Was the name Patti Jakowski?" Carter's voice increased several decibels.

"Yes, that was it." He stopped talking for a moment, and then narrowed his eyes at the men. "And then she asked the strangest question. She was with her friend, Mr. Hamed, and she asked Carrie for his first name. Carrie told me she thought Ms. Jakowski looked scared."

Carter stood on the sidewalk seething. "And it didn't occur to you that maybe you should call the police, or the FBI?"

"Well...I...uh." Robert wiped at the sweat trickling down his face. "Guess I made a mistake."

Carter glared at the man.

"You said the other FBI agent left instructions to call if Ms. Jakowski came back home."

Robert blinked rapidly and his Adam's apple bobbed up and down. He didn't say anything for a few moments. "Ms. Jakowski said everything had been taken care of and so there was no reason to call."

"Do you know where she went?" Carter was anxious.

Robert looked at Carter, much preferring his question to Marcus's. "Mmmm. She said something about some kind of charity function. She was all dressed up. She looked great."

"What charity function?" Marcus asked.

"I don't rememb...wait a minute." He looked at the two men blankly. "But I can't remember. I wasn't really listening. I was trying to figure out why she signed someone else's name."

"Think, Robert. This woman is in big trouble. We've got to find her before she gets herself killed." Carter wanted to shake the man to make him remember.

Robert's eyes bugged and the blood drained from his face. "I can't remember. I'm sorry. If I could remember, I'd...hey, wait a minute, Carrie was there, too. Maybe she can remember. Let me go call her."

Carter let out a breath.

Finally, something going their way.

In less than five minutes, they were on their way to the Children's Fund benefit.

30

She'd blown it.

Patti stared at the drink she'd taken from Joseph without a thought. Her heart raced and sweat pooled in her palms. If she'd fooled Joseph at all, he certainly knew something was off-kilter now.

It hadn't occurred to her Jamie wouldn't drink, but it made sense.

Jamie needed to keep her mind focused when she was around these people. Or maybe her sister had developed an alcohol problem.

Either way, it didn't matter.

What mattered was Patti had made a major blunder. It was imperative to get off the yacht.

Joseph had been scary, but compared to his brother, he was a pussycat. Looking into Raymond's black eyes, she'd felt evil in the man.

Suzanne was still mindlessly chattering away.

As Patti thought back to the whispered conference she'd seen take place between Joseph and Dennis, she couldn't help but wonder if Suzanne was part of the plot.

Patti stood and Suzanne jumped up as well.

"I'm going to the restroom," Patti explained.

"I'll go with you."

"Not necessary, Suzanne," Patti said firmly. Then she smiled. "Really, I can handle being alone that long."

Suzanne looked worried. "No, I have to go with you."

"What do you mean you have to go with me?"

Suzanne flushed and stammered an explanation. "Be...because Dennis told me to stay with you."

Patti's heart almost jumped out of her chest. "Why?"

"I don't know. He told me to stay with you and not to let you leave."

"That's just ridiculous, Suzanne. I'm quite capable of going to the bathroom, or anywhere else I choose, without you watching me. Don't worry so much. Go have fun. This is a party, isn't it?"

Suzanne looked around as though searching for someone who could help her decide what to do. "You promise you're coming right back?"

Without answering, Patti waved as she threaded her way through the throng.

Taking a final glance at Suzanne, Patti could see she was already hunting for Joseph or Dennis.

The woman might be Jamie's friend, but she wasn't willing to risk Dennis's wrath.

The engines of the yacht started up. The floor vibrated beneath her feet.

Panic seized Patti.

If the yacht left before she could get off, she'd be in big trouble. If only Carter was here.

She broke into a slow jog, not bothering to say 'excuse me' to people as she bumped into them.

It was getting hard to breathe. The heat from the people pressing in threatened to strangle her.

Laughing and having a good time. No idea of the danger.

The music blared, but she could still hear her heart

throbbing in spite of the noise.

It seemed like forever, but she slipped through a door and the warm salty breeze caressed her face. Taking a deep breath of the ocean air, tension oozed out.

Almost there. All I have to do is find the exit and I'll be safe.

There were less people out on the deck than in the ballroom and it was quieter. She could breathe again.

She played back the layout of the yacht and turned to the right. If she was correct, she'd be off the ship in a minute.

As she turned the corner, Raymond Hammond stood in front of her talking with a group of men. His back was turned.

Patti's feet froze. If Raymond saw her, he wouldn't let her leave. She turned her back to Raymond and headed back the other way.

"Jamie, hold on a minute," Raymond called to her.

She turned with a smile and gave a small wave. "I'm looking for Joseph." She called back over her shoulder as she kept walking. "I'll be back in a minute."

Without looking, she hiked off in the other direction as fast as her legs would let her.

Within moments, Raymond was beside her and grabbed hold of her elbow. He smirked. His eyes were cold and hard.

Her pulse raced.

"No reason to do that, Jamie." Patti didn't like the way he said Jamie's name. "I know exactly where Joseph is. After all, he is my brother, as you well know. I'll be glad to take you to him."

"You don't have to do that. I'm sure I can find him

on my own, and you probably have important business to take care of." She twisted away, but his hand remained on her arm. She tried again to slip from his grasp, but failed.

He pressed his thumb and forefinger into her arm until it became painful.

Tears sprang to her eyes.

"It's no bother at all. I was going that way, anyway."

Patti abandoned all sense of politeness. "Let go of me, Raymond." Her voice was rising. "Or I'll start screaming and ruin all your little plans."

Heads turned.

"I don't think so, Patti. Oh, I'm sorry, I mean Jamie." His eyes grew dark and rage shone in them. "No, I think I was right the first time, Patti. I don't know what game you're playing, but I suggest you come along quietly unless you want me to kill Jamie."

Hope leapt up in Patti.

Jamie was alive.

"Where is she? Is she here?"

Fanatical rage shone in his eyes. "All in good time. If you would like to see her, come with me. If you don't, you are free to go, but then I kill her. Your choice, Patti." His whispered words sounded like a snake hissing just before striking its prey.

She didn't dare make a scene.

Raymond would do as he'd threatened.

Nodding, she continued to walk with him.

The first glimmer of hope she'd had in days sparked in her heart.

Jamie was alive.

Raymond led her to a door. As he closed it the noise from the crowd and the sunlight dimmed.

A chill went down her spine. She was alone with this terrorist. Her feet slowed as he forced her down the steps.

At the bottom of the steps was a hallway with several doors.

He stopped at the second door and turned to Patti. "Inside." He opened the door.

Don't do it. Patti could almost hear Jamie yelling the words.

Patti took a step as if to enter the room, but instead she turned and pushed Raymond as hard as she could.

He fell back and without a moment's hesitation, she ran. *Had to get back up on deck with people.*

Patti pushed down the panic bubbling up and sprinted towards the exit. *Almost there.* The steps were in front of her. Just a few more feet.

A pair of hands grabbed her by the hair and dragged her backwards away from the steps.

She turned to fight, but Raymond pinned her arms and spun her around. He held her neck with one arm and her arms with the other as he dragged her backwards.

She screamed as loud as she could, but the hall was empty. Refusing to give up, she continued to struggle, turning in his clutches as she tried to lash out.

Raymond slapped her.

She sagged and saw stars. Blood trickled from her lip.

"Shut up."

As he pushed her into the room, she toppled to the floor.

The lurch of the ship announced the beginning of its journey to the open ocean.

≈∞≪

With Marcus driving like a maniac, they made it to the marina.

Carter couldn't believe the madhouse in front of them.

Limos lined both sides of the streets. Throngs of people were walking on the sidewalks and overflowed into the streets, making it almost impossible to drive. The media trucks and cameras only added to the confusion.

They'd never find Patti in this mess.

Marcus parked illegally, and they jumped out of the car. Searching the crowd, Carter spied a man with a Port Authority uniform. He nudged Marcus.

They walked up to him.

"FBI." Marcus announced and held out his badge.

The man examined it and looked back up at Marcus. "What can I do for you?"

"We're looking for the Children's Fund benefit. It's on some yacht around here."

The man nodded. "It was." He pointed at a speck far out in the harbor. "That's probably it. If you were supposed to help out with security, you missed the boat." The man laughed at his own joke.

Carter wanted to put his fist through something. *This was bad news.*

Patti was out on the ocean with terrorists who wanted her dead.

His stomach churned. *Please, God, don't let this happen.*

"Where's the harbormaster? We need to see him now," Marcus barked.

The man came to attention and stood straighter.

"Sure, sure. No problem. Come with me."

The harbormaster's office was a brick building located near the water.

The three men walked in, but were stopped by his assistant. A placard sitting on her desk identified her as Evelyn. She informed them her boss would be back soon and they could sit over there to wait for him to return.

"That's not acceptable. We've got a life and death situation on the yacht with the Children's Fund benefit party on it. We've got to get that boat back to the dock," Carter told the woman. "You find your boss now."

She arched a well-groomed eyebrow at him. "I'm sure that's an exaggeration and even if it's not, there isn't anything he can do. That's a private yacht. We can't make them come back in."

"Are you telling me, Evelyn, if you received information there was a bomb on that boat, you couldn't make them come back in?" Carter fired back.

She glared at Carter. "That's what I'm telling you."

"What if I told you there was terrorist activity going on?"

Evelyn looked at Carter as if he might be nuts. "I suppose we could suggest they come back in, but..." She gave an exaggerated shrug.

A short red-headed man walked in the room.

The secretary stood and looked at her boss. "These men want to talk with you. Apparently, they think—"

"That's OK." Carter interrupted, "We'll tell him what we think."

Marcus identified himself as FBI.

"We've got a serious situation on the Children's Fund benefit yacht out there. We need to get the yacht back to port. Do you have the authority? If not, you need to call—" Carter asked before Marcus could talk.

"I have the authority." The man nodded. "As long as they haven't made it out to international waters yet, I can."

"And what if they're in international waters?" Carter asked.

"Then, we've got a problem."

31

Patti tumbled to the floor and looked around frantically. Just as she suspected, no Jamie.

But Joseph Hamed sat on the couch with his head hung low, staring at his shoes.

Raymond waved his hands in an expansive welcoming motion. "Welcome to the Ronald Reagan State Room. It is so named because the former president once stayed in this very room as a guest of Kathryn's parents. And now you're the honored guest." He laughed. "Isn't America a wonderful place?"

He kicked her in the side.

Gasping, she held her side and stayed on the floor.

Along with Joseph, two men in security uniforms stood at attention near the bar, as if waiting for orders.

Patti had no doubt what their orders would be.

Joseph got up from the sofa and stepped forward, his tanned face mottled with anger. He spit out his next words. "Did you think you could fool me, Patti? Did you suppose I wouldn't know the difference?"

"I just wanted to find Jamie. How can you let him hurt me?" Patti cried. "If you loved Jamie, you would help me find out what happened to her."

A look of pain crossed Joseph's face, but only for a moment. His next words were as angry as his eyes. "Jamie betrayed me. She didn't love me. She was using me to get information for your corrupt government. If I had known, I would have killed her myself and enjoyed it."

"I thought you loved her," she yelled at him.

Something flickered in his eyes, but it died out with Joseph's next words. "I loved nothing about her. She was a weak, despicable woman. I am glad my brother did what he did." He sneered at her.

Raymond smirked, but his black eyes were void of any emotion. "Of course, I would have enjoyed doing it myself but from what I heard, she suffered greatly before she died."

Her heart shattered. Jumping up, she rushed at Raymond, slapping at him.

Raymond pushed her back, laughing as he did.

One of the officers stepped forward and before she knew what was happening, the man threw her to the floor.

The other officer descended on Patti, carrying duct tape. As he reached for Patti's feet, she kicked him as hard as she could in his face.

Blood gushed from his nose as he crumpled to the floor with a moan.

The other guard wasted no time, grabbing her hands to tape them, and then covering her mouth with more tape.

Raymond Hammond came toward Patti with a fire in his eyes that warned of danger.

She cowered.

The look on his face said he might kill her right then. Grabbing her by the hair, he lifted her up in one swift movement.

She moaned through the duct tape.

He pulled back his fist and hit her.

She felt the pain, saw sparks of light, and then

darkness.

> ᔆᔆ

Patti heard voices and fought her way back to consciousness. Her hands and feet were bound, and the tape was still on her mouth so she couldn't scream for help. Lying on the sofa, her hands had been pushed through the slats of the mission style sofa and then taped again. No way was she getting away from these mad men.

God, be with me. Patti repeated the mantra again and again. Strength and calmness poured into her spirit. Whatever was going to happen was going to happen, but God loved her.

The Lord had her back.

She opened her eyes.

Only Joseph and Raymond remained. Their backs were turned to her as they leaned up against the bar.

Raymond clasped his brother by the shoulder. "Things are going as planned, Joseph. It won't be long now. Everything is in place."

"Everything?"

Raymond paced the room. "The formula arrived and is locked in my basement. We will begin distribution over the next few weeks and on the specified date, it will happen the way we've planned."

"That is good. It will destroy this country's economic system." Joseph nodded, a joyful glee in his eyes. "And destroy their peace of mind as well. These Americans are arrogant. They believe nothing can destroy their country, their excessive lifestyle, their precious freedom. But they will soon discover how wrong they are."

"Soon I will have avenged my wife and my child."

Joseph's head whipped around towards his brother. His face was a combination of concern and surprise. "Rahmed, this is not revenge. This is—"

Rahmed made a dismissive gesture. "I know, Joseph, but you can't understand. You never loved a woman the way I loved my wife. The soldiers killed her and our unborn child. This country must pay. You cannot understand such things."

Joseph faced his brother, his face flushed and his fists curled in a ball.

A surge of hope grew in Patti. If the two men had a falling out, it could be the break she needed.

Joseph walked closer to his brother, his fists by his sides.

Hit him, hit him.

His voice was low and angry. "I do understand such things. This was the kind of love I had for Jamie, but you killed her. I accept it was necessary, but do not tell me I have not loved in such a way."

Raymond took a step back and patted Joseph's arm. "Of course, brother. I meant no disrespect. I was merely pointing out personal revenge is sweet, indeed. Especially when it furthers our cause."

Joseph nodded.

Her heart sank.

"What now?" Joseph asked his brother.

Raymond looked towards Patti.

She willed herself to not move.

"No one knows she is here. We will simply throw her overboard. She'll disappear into the ocean, never to be a problem for me or for you again." As he talked, he pointed to a glass door leading to a small balcony.

"As long as no one sees us."

"It should not be a problem. It is a private balcony. That is my plan for Maria as well. I can be the grieving widower and keep my cover in place. And as mourners stop by to express their condolences, they will leave with a bit more than what they arrived with. It will be the perfect way to deliver the virus formula. It will work out well."

Rahmed was planning on killing his own wife to further his cause. A heartless monster.

Joseph nodded. "It might work, but what if the FBI knows more than we believe?"

She saw a chance and she took it. She struggled until the men noticed her.

Both men gaped at her as if they'd forgotten she was there.

"Take the tape off her mouth," Raymond told Joseph. He showed her the gun in his hand. "If you scream, I will shoot you. It has a silencer, so no one will be the wiser. No one is going to come rescue you."

Patti nodded.

Joseph tore the tape off her mouth.

She winced as it tore delicate skin, but refused to give Raymond or Joseph the satisfaction of showing it hurt.

Raymond sneered at Patti as if he hoped she would scream. He wanted an excuse to shoot her. "Do you have something you want to say to me?"

"Do you really think I'm dumb enough to come by myself? Of course, the FBI knows I'm here. They're on the ship, too."

Raymond Hammond stepped closer, his eyes narrowed as he watched her. "Is this the truth?"

She had to make him believe it. "Of course, it's the

truth. They wanted to know your name and now they do, Raymond Hammond. You made a mistake when you took Jamie." She willed herself to meet his eyes. If she could convince him, she might still have a chance.

His face darkened with anger. "Where are these imaginary agents?" He motioned around the room. "I don't see them. I don't hear them barging down the hall to rescue you." Raymond sat down on the chair beside her and looked into her eyes for several long moments. "You are a very brave woman, but your eyes tell me you are lying." He grabbed a handful of her hair and pulled.

It brought tears to her eyes. She bit her lip to keep from yelling out.

"I do not like people to lie to me."

Patti stared hard at the despicable man. "Do my eyes also tell you that you are about to be arrested? Just let me go and I will help you turn yourself in so no one gets hurt."

Raymond chuckled. "That sounds like a line from one of your bad American movies." He continued to laugh.

Patti's face felt hot and she knew it was bright red. "Think what you want. They will be along any moment," she said, trying to sound as if she weren't worried.

"I shall." He pulled her hair again.

She moaned in spite of herself.

He looked at Joseph. "I think she is lying. No one knows she is here. We will throw them both overboard. The authorities will find a suicide note at home explaining everything." He laughed.

Patti had to make Raymond believe she wasn't alone of the ship. "Really? Joseph? Didn't you tell your brother we were stopped by the police on the way here? What do you think it was all about?"

Raymond jerked his head towards Joseph.

Neither man was laughing any longer.

"Is this true?"

Joseph spoke slowly. "Yes, we were stopped, but it was a routine traffic stop."

"Are you sure about that?" she blurted out.

"I am sure," Joseph said. "She did not talk to anyone. There would have been no point in stopping us. That would have made me suspicious."

Raymond looked back at Patti. He shrugged. "Oh, well. Good try. We should go up and make our presence known. The next time I come in the room, it will be time for you to die like your sister."

His eyes glittered with hatred. Raymond placed the duct tape back on her mouth.

Patti glared at him.

"Is this what you came here for? To find your sister's killer? You have found him and what did it get you? I was willing to let her child live, but that wasn't enough for you. You will die as your sister did, and for no good reason."

Joseph looked at his brother, surprise etched on his face. "A child? Jamie had a child?"

A strange expression crossed Raymond's face and then it was gone. "Yes, the traitor had a child."

"I did not know this."

Rahmed turned to his brother, his voice disgusted. "There was much you didn't know about this woman. You did not know she had a twin sister. You did not know she worked for the FBI. That is why she had to die. She tricked you into giving her information that could hurt me. Hurt the movement."

"Who is the child's father?" Joseph asked.

A look of distaste was on Raymond's face. "Who knows? These American women are so promiscuous. Be assured, you are not the father, Joseph. You have only known her for several months and the child is much older."

"That is not true. I never told you, but I knew Jamie before, Rahmed, when I was in New York City."

Raymond's face turned hard and angry. "Forget about this woman and her child. They are nothing to us. I did what I had to do."

"Of course, I believe you." Joseph showed no hesitation and Patti's heart sank.

He wouldn't help her.

Patti tried to jump off the couch, but couldn't.

Raymond sneered at her and put a hand on Joseph's shoulder. "We must go on deck and mingle and be seen. No need to worry. I will bring Maria here and we can take care of both of these problems for good."

He killed Jamie and he meant to kill her, and then his own wife.

He was a monster. He needed to be stopped.

32

Carter paced up and down the pier. The yacht was nowhere in sight, but the harbormaster assured them it would be back to port soon.

In the meantime, Patti's life wouldn't be worth two cents if the terrorists figured out she wasn't Jamie.

Marcus walked up to him with cell phone in hand. "They're on their way back. Forty-five minutes. An hour at the most."

"No way. We can't wait that long. We've got to get on that ship before that."

"Don't worry. There are more agents on the way. We aren't going to let these guys get away from us. We're going to nail them."

Marcus was more interested in arresting the terrorists than Patti's safety.

"Every minute we aren't on that ship, is one more minute she may be killed. That's my concern. My only concern."

"I'm worried about her, too."

"Apparently not enough to do anything," Carter pointed out at the bay. "We've got to get a boat and get out there. Now. If you can't arrange it, I will."

෪෧

Patti stared up at the ceiling of the stateroom. To keep from panicking, she prayed and kept her mind focused on the good things in her life. Sabrina. Tears trickled down her cheek. Poor Sabrina. She'd have no one now, except Anna. The tears came faster.

Carter and his smile flashed in her mind's eye. It was hard to believe she'd met him such a short time ago. He'd done his best to keep her safe, but she'd been too stubborn.

The door opened.

Maria Hammond walked in.

What was she? Show and Tell?

Raymond must have found a way to lure Maria there. In a matter of minutes, both of them would be dead and thrown into the ocean.

She leaned down to Patti. "Don't be afraid. I'm here to help you," She pulled the tape off Patti's mouth.

Patti took a gasp of fresh air, and then spoke. "We've got to get out of here before they come back. He's going to kill both of us. He wants to kill—"

Maria nodded. "I was standing at the window. I heard it all." She had a kitchen knife in her hands and she used it to cut the tape binding Patti's arms and legs.

"Where's my purse?" Patti asked as she looked around wildly. "I've got a gun and a cell phone. We've got to call for help." Patti grabbed her purse from the corner where Raymond had thrown it and pulled the cell phone out. "Let me call for help."

"Not here." Maria shook her head. "We don't have time. We've got to get out of this room before they come back."

"We need a place to hide."

"I know the yacht. Let's go."

They ran to the door.

Patti's hand reached out to grab the knob. In the same moment the door opened and one of the security guards walked in.

Patti froze.

The man's mouth fell open in shock when he saw Patti and Maria. He moved towards them with his gun drawn.

Maria grabbed a chair and hit the man with all the strength she could muster.

He moaned but didn't go down. Instead, he grabbed the chair and wrenched it from her grip.

Maria stepped forward, but with an uncanny sense the man turned as she lifted a lamp to hit him.

He moved out of the way as her arms came down.

The swing knocked her off balance and she fell to the floor. Maria scrambled back to her feet, but the man was quicker and before either of the women could stop him, he had Maria in his grasp and a gun to her head.

Maria looked as terrified as Patti felt.

The security guard wiggled the gun still pressed against Maria's head.

All of them gasped for breath.

"Be a good girl and I won't kill her yet. That was a nice try," he told Maria. "But not good enough." He sucked in more air.

"Don't listen to him." Maria screamed at her. "Run. Get out of here and go get help."

Patti looked into the man's eyes and knew he would do exactly what he promised. She had one more chance. If she had the courage.

Patti clutched her purse. Turning slightly so he couldn't see, she slipped Jamie's gun out of the purse.

She'd never shot a gun in her life.

The guard was looking down at Maria, who still struggled.

Patti threw her purse as hard as she could.

As he turned to look behind him, his hold on Maria loosened.

She pushed at Maria, but he didn't let go of the woman. Patti shoved the gun into his back. She pulled the trigger but nothing happened.

The man turned back. He laughed, grabbed the gun and tossed it to the floor.

Patti slapped at the man, but he kicked her in the stomach. She crumpled to the floor moaning.

Grabbing Patti by the hair, he forced her to look up at him. "If you so much as move a muscle, I will shoot her. Do you understand me?"

Patti nodded. She watched as he moved Maria to the sofa and pressed the gun to her head.

He handed her the duct tape. "Wrap it around your feet and the sofa leg." His gun didn't waver from Maria's head. His gaze never left Patti.

She couldn't risk moving or he'd kill Maria.

He pulled her to the chair and hit her hard enough to make her head swim. She was duct-taped within minutes.

"Much better. I don't think you'll be getting loose again." He walked out the door.

Maria's body shook as she sobbed.

Patti jerked her arms and legs, looking for a weak spot, but stopped when she realized it was useless.

She heard a noise at the door and then it opened.

Joseph Hamed walked over to them.

Time to die.

So much she'd wanted to do. She'd never marry,

never have a child of her own, or even experience real love with a man. Her stomach heaved but she steeled herself, determined to die with dignity. She prayed, asking God to shelter Sabrina.

Joseph stared down at her with an intensity that made her pulse race. "I am going to take the tape off. Do not scream." He pulled out a gun and pointed it at Maria. "If you scream, I will shoot her, but you will still tell me what I want to know. Understand?"

Patti nodded.

He pulled the tape off her mouth.

"I want information regarding this child of Jamie's," he demanded. "And I want the truth. If you lie to me, I will shoot you in the head and be done with you."

Patti would never let this man know Sabrina was his daughter. Sabrina had to be protected from him at all costs. It would probably be the last thing she did, but maybe the best.

She nodded. "Yes, I understand."

"How old is she?"

Patti wondered how long Joseph had known Jamie. "Seven years old."

He backhanded her.

Patti's head snapped back and she saw stars. Blood oozed from her lip.

"You're lying. I will give you one more chance and then she will die." He placed the gun to Maria's head.

He would kill the woman if Patti didn't tell him the truth.

In her letter, Jamie had begged her not to let this man know Sabrina was his child. But Jamie wouldn't want Patti to let this woman be killed, either.

Forgive me, Jamie. I can't let this woman die. Patti cast

her eyes down in surrender.

Joseph Hamed must have seen the defeat and he smiled with satisfaction. "How old is the girl?"

Patti whispered the answer. "Four years old."

"When is her birthday?"

"I don't know. I didn't know she existed until a week ago."

"What does she look like?"

She wanted to lie to him. She didn't want this man to know he had a daughter. "She's beautiful. She has black hair, an olive complexion, and dark eyes."

"Is she my daughter?"

Long moments passed.

He waited.

"I don't know for sure," Patti finally answered. "But I assume you are most likely her father."

Joseph closed his eyes. An internal battle raged inside that showed on his face. When he opened them, his eyes were filled with pain, but resolution shone in them. "I will help you. You must keep my daughter safe and help her to have a happy life. You will do this."

"Of course," Patti managed to answer in spite of her shock.

"Jamie and I loved each other, no matter what you might think. We were planning a life together. Jamie made me see violence is wrong and not the answer to my country's political problems. We were in love. It is too late for me and for Jamie, but you can keep my daughter safe. Give her a happy life."

Patti stared at Joseph, not sure if she could trust him.

"Now you must go and hide. When we dock, slip out with the other people and leave here. You must take her somewhere where they cannot find you. That is the only way you will be safe."

"I will. I will." Patti bit back tears.

"Take care of my daughter," Joseph said. "Give her a good life."

He bent down to undo Patti's tape from around her wrists. When Patti's hands were free, he turned from her and pulled the tape from Maria.

Patti quickly bent down and pulled the tape off her own ankles, and then Maria's.

Patti turned to thank the man, but he pushed the women toward the door. "Go, just go. Get out of here, now," he hissed.

"What about Layla?" Maria asked. "What about my daughter?"

Joseph nodded as if coming to a decision. "Raymond said she was still with her little friend. That is all I know. Let me check the hall, then you must go hide."

Joseph opened the door. "Raymond."

No time to think.

Patti grabbed Maria's hand and pulled her into the bathroom. Patti watched the brothers through the door, waiting for a chance to escape.

Joseph opened the front door wider. "Raymond. It is good you are here. They are gone. They have escaped."

"What do you mean?"Raymond asked.

Joseph motioned backwards into the empty room. "They are gone. Mason told me he found Maria trying to help Patti escape. I came in to check on them, and this is what I found. Perhaps Patti was telling the truth. Perhaps the FBI are on board. They have to be, how else could she have escaped? Mason assured me they were secure."

Raymond punched the door. He pushed past Joseph and rushed into the room.

Joseph followed.

"I do not believe this. If the FBI had found them, we would both be under arrest right now. Someone helped them escape."

Raymond bent down and looked at the door lock. "This hasn't been tampered with. That means someone who had a key helped them." Clearly angry, Raymond stood and stared at his brother with unblinking eyes.

Patti's pulse raced. She was sure Raymond heard her heart pounding. She forced herself to slow down her breathing. If she had an anxiety attack now, they would both die.

Raymond spoke slowly and deliberately. "There are only a few people with keys."

With a grim smile Joseph said, "Good. That will narrow our list of suspects."

Raymond continued to stare at Joseph, his black eyes glittering. "Yes, but I can think of one who would have a motive to help them."

"Who would that be?"

Raymond lifted his gun and aimed it at Joseph. "That would be you, my brother."

Joseph threw his hands in the air as if shocked by the accusation. "Have you lost your mind, Rahmed? You are my brother. You know how committed I am to our cause. I have given my life for it. We have worked side by side for many years. How can you think I betrayed you, or the cause?"

"Because you loved the American woman." Raymond spit out the words as if they were distasteful to him. "That woman, Jamie. You were willing to betray us for her. I saw the look in your eyes when you heard there was a child."

When Joseph spoke, his voice was tinged with panic. "Never. Never would I betray you, Rahmed. Yes, I wanted to quit, but never would I betray you or the movement. Had I known she was FBI, I would have killed her myself. I would never betray you, my brother."

"I know nothing of the sort."

"We don't have time for this—"

Without warning, Raymond pushed Joseph to the floor. Raymond closed the door and turned back to Joseph. Raymond's black eyes glittered with hatred.

"Rahmed, please, we are..." Joseph implored his brother.

Raymond walked towards him.

Joseph scooted on the floor trying to get away. "Rahmed, don't do--"

Raymond lifted the gun and pulled the trigger.

Patti's hand flew to her mouth to stifle her scream.

Maria's nails dug into her palm.

Raymond stood watching his brother die. Stepping over Joseph, he spat out, "traitor." He walked out of the room.

Patti and Maria stared at each other, but said nothing.

After a few minutes, Patti nodded at Maria and the two women bolted through the bathroom door.

Patti was intent on getting to the stairs and among the partygoers. Too afraid to go to the security guards or the captain, they both agreed they couldn't trust anyone.

Not that she would feel safe until she was off the yacht and far away from Raymond.

Maria stopped Patti at the steps. "We can't just go up there. We're a mess. They'll be sure to discover us. We've got to find somewhere to hide."

Patti saw the truth in Maria's words. "Sometimes the best place to hide is right out in the open." She looked at Maria and repeated the words.

Maria nodded in agreement. "That's it. I've got an idea."

Maria led them down another hallway and pointed at a door.

Patti's first impulse was to stay out of rooms where she could once again be trapped.

Maria grabbed her arm and pulled her through. The room was empty except for clothes.

"This is the female servers' lounge. We can hide in here until the yacht docks. Raymond would never look for us here."

The servers had changed into their costumes in the room. Clothing was everywhere. In addition to their street clothes, there were extra serving costumes, wigs, and other beauty aids.

"Sounds good." Patti turned to Maria. "I don't understand. Why does your husband want to kill you?"

"I figured out he was involved in something horrible." Her dark brown eyes filled with tears and her lips trembled. "It sounds crazy, but I think he's a terrorist."

"He is."

"Before I could call the cops, he stole my daughter," Maria said through tears. "He told me if I didn't do exactly what he wanted, I would never see her again." She took a breath and continued. "He told me I could see Layla after the party, but it was a lie. He was going to kill me – just like he was going to kill you. Why was he calling you Patti? I thought your name was Jamie."

Hearing Jamie's name brought back the grief.

"Jamie is my twin sister. I came looking for her and ended up here." She took out her cell phone then scrolled down to find Carter Caldwell's number. "Hurry. Hurry," Patti whispered as the phone rang and rang. *Please let him answer the phone. Please.* "Pick up. Pick up."

"Hello."

At the sound of his voice, Patti almost fell apart. "Carter. Carter, is that you? It's me Patti," she whispered into the phone. She longed for the safety of his arms around her.

More static.

"Patti, is that you? I can barely hear you. Are you Ok? Where are you?"

"I can't hear. We've got a bad connection, just listen, Carter. We need help. I can't explain all of it so listen. I'm on this yacht in San Francisco. You've got to get some police here to help me. He wants to kill—"

"Patti, I know..."

Patti couldn't make out his words over the static. She hoped he could hear her. "You've got to get someone to the ship. I don't know the name of it, but it's the Children's Fund benefit. I know you're in Palm Beach, but call Marcus. He'll know what to do."

Patti struggled to make out his words but the static was louder than his voice. "I can't hear you, Carter. I can't make out what you're saying."

Silence. The static stopped along with the connection.

"It was such a bad connection I couldn't tell if he

understood what I was saying or not. I guess we better plan on taking care of ourselves."

Maria looked around the room. "We could hide in here, but if they find us then we've got no way to escape. I say we should make ourselves presentable and try to mingle with the others. Just be sure we stay together and away from Raymond."

Patti's gaze wandered around the room filled with servers' costumes and leis. An idea formed in her mind.

It might just work.

33

The police speedboat was racing towards the yacht when the call from Patti came.

Carter tried to reconnect but the line went dead.

Marcus sat watching him. "What did she say?"

"It was a bad connection, but I did hear her say something about the Children's Fund benefit. She's got to be on that ship, why else would she talk about it? I tried to tell her we would be boarding the ship in a few minutes, but I don't think she could hear me. Too much static. She sounded terrified, but she's still alive. Thank God."

Marcus flipped open his phone. "Hanks here." A pause. "When? Marcus's face paled. "How?" Marcus closed his eyes, pinched the bridge of his nose with his free hand. "Has it been confirmed?" Marcus listened, no expression on his face, with eyes still closed.

The grief on the man's face was evident.

Marcus took a deep breath. "I see. That makes sense to me, as well. We're on our way to the yacht now. The situation should be contained soon." He flipped the phone shut.

Carter waited.

After a moment Marcus looked over at him. "They found Jamie."

"Alive or dead?"

"Dead. Some tourists found her body in the

Glades."

Patti would be devastated. And the thought of cute little Sabrina growing up without her mother was the worst part of it.

"Of course, that's where every murderer in Florida takes the body. A positive identification was made?"

"Not yet. Can't get fingerprints or use dental records, but she fits Jamie's general description. Right height, weight, and hair color."

"Maybe they're wrong. Maybe it's someone else."

"Yeah, what are the chances of that?" Marcus lifted his gaze from the cell phone he still held.

"Not much of a chance, but—"

"They were going to take a DNA sample from Sabrina but decided it would be less intrusive to get the sample from Patti, since they are twins. They're going to wait for a final ID until she gets back to Florida."

"I'm sorry, Marcus. I know she was a friend—"

Marcus held up a hand and shook his head. "Not now. Let's stay focused on keeping Patti alive."

જ∾જ

The police boat sprayed up water as it came to a halt next to the yacht.

Carter and Marcus boarded, along with two other FBI agents.

The partygoers stopped what they were doing to stare at the group who'd made such a dramatic entrance on to the ship.

Carter searched for Patti.

The captain and another man dressed in a white linen suit and a fedora walked towards them. Neither looked happy about their intrusion.

Mr. Fedora stepped forward. "I'm Harold Hart. I own this ship. What is the meaning of this? We're on our way back as asked. We were told the matter would be handled discreetly. You can't simply come aboard and ruin the party. These people have—"

Carter stepped close to the man. "You've got big trouble. I suggest you cooperate or we might think you're part of the terrorist ring we'll be arresting soon."

Harold Hart flinched and backed away from Carter. He looked at Marcus. "What is he talking about?"

"We don't have time to explain," Carter answered. "We need to find Joseph Hamed, Jamie Jakowski, and anyone else who knows the two of them. What's the best way to do that?"

"Look, you will take the time to tell me what's going on, or you can get off my yacht."

"You are in American waters." Carter said. "Do you want to be responsible for someone's death? Because right now, you can be arrested for obstruction of justice."

Marcus stepped between the two men and spoke softly. "Let's calm down and go somewhere with more privacy."

"You go talk. I'm going to look for Patti." Carter said.

"Carter. We've got to do this in an organized way. Otherwise, we're wasting our time.

Looking for Patti would have to wait a few more minutes.

Carter hoped it wouldn't be too late.

❧◊

Patti and Maria were dressed in identical brightly colored Hawaiian shirts, white shorts and long, black wigs, making them indistinguishable from the other servers. Heavy makeup hid even more.

Maria's blue sandals with long straps that crisscrossed to her mid-calf were noticeable, however. Patti's simple white sandals blended in with the server's outfit she wore.

"Raymond won't even think to look at the serving staff. He's too arrogant. As far as he's concerned, they aren't even people, just robots put there to serve him."

"I guess we should both find a tray to carry and then make our way to the exit ramp."

"Hold on a minute." Maria looked around the room. She walked over to the sink area and found a piece of paper. She wrote something down and brought it back to Patti. "Here's the address where I think my daughter is. If...if something happens to me, find her. Don't let that monster near her. Promise me."

"I promise." She touched Maria's arm. "I need a moment to pray."

Maria nodded. "Go ahead. We need all the help we can get."

Patti extended a hand to Maria. "Pray with me."

She backed away. "It's been so long since I've prayed. God doesn't care what I want."

Thinking back to what Carter had told her, Patti gave her a gentle smile and grabbed hold of her hand. "Not true. God's mercies are new each day. He'll hear us and He'll help us."

They knelt down. When they were finished, both

women wiped away their tears, ready to face their future. If they had one on this earth.

∂∾∾∽

Patti held a tray of drinks as she roved through the crowd, but her eyes never left Maria who passed out appetizers a few feet from her.

Maria whispered to Patti. "I heard some people talking. They said a group of men boarded the boat. H.H. argued with them and the group disappeared. Who do you think it was?"

Patti's heart lurched with hope. "Must be the police or FBI. Carter must have been able to get hold of Marcus. We've got to find them. They're probably looking for me. Did those people say where they were?"

Maria shook her head and looked towards shore. "It won't be long until we'll be back to the pier. People are saying H. H. was asked to come back. No one knows why. You go search for them, but as soon as the yacht docks, I'm leaving. I can't risk letting Raymond get to Layla before I do. If that happens, I will never see her again."

Raymond had, no doubt, already made a phone call to the people holding Maria's daughter, but there was no point in telling Maria. If she lost hope, she might fall completely apart and that wouldn't be good.

"We'll tell the police and they can dispatch a car to her right away. It will be quicker than us going alone."

"Good. You do that, but I'm still getting off the ship to go find Layla. I gue..." Maria stopped speaking midsentence. The blood drained from her face, replaced by a look of terror.

Patti turned to see Raymond. He was searching the crowd.

Patti grabbed Maria and both turned their backs.

ॐ

Carter stared down at the body of Joseph Hamed in the Ronald Reagan State Room.

The Special Agent-In-Charge was barking orders into his cell phone a few feet away.

Kathryn sobbed as her husband helped her to a chair. "I can't believe this. Who would do something like this?"

Marcus looked at Mason Fredricks, the head of the security force, who'd been hired for the event. "So, no one reported hearing gunshots?"

He shook his head.

Carter looked at the amount of duct tape scattered around the room. It was obvious it had been used to subdue someone, probably Patti. But, maybe not just Patti. Too much tape for just one person.

Carter's mind raced through scenarios.

Kathryn interrupted Carter's thoughts. "I don't understand. Joseph Hamed was a terrorist? I can't believe it. We've known him for years."

"Impossible. Impossible," muttered H.H. but he looked as if he might faint. He sat down beside his wife and looked up at Carter. "What do you want us to do?"

The agent slammed his phone shut and walked over to the group. He looked at H.H. and then at Mason Fredricks. "Call your security force together. Have them move everyone into a ballroom, and then lock down each of the ballrooms. Don't let anyone leave a room once it's been locked down. Do you have enough men to guard the doors and get the others in the rooms?"

Mason nodded. "Not a problem."

"Are those the only places where the parties are being held? In the ballrooms and on deck?" Marcus asked Kathryn Hart.

She nodded. "Yes, but we didn't actually shut off the other areas. We locked the private rooms so people couldn't snoop around them, but they're free to walk around."

"Good. Then it shouldn't be too hard to contain them." Marcus nodded, and then looked at Carter and the other agent. "While the security force is securing the areas, we'll make a search of the rest of the yacht."

⤞⤝

"What do you think is going on?" Patti asked Maria.

Men dressed in security uniforms approached partygoers and asked them to go into the ballrooms. Remembering the security men in the stateroom, Patti had no intention of following them anywhere. She and Maria would need to find a place to hide before Raymond and his goons found them.

"I don't know, but I don't like it." Maria set down the tray she'd been holding. "It might be a trap Raymond's set. We don't really know if the FBI came aboard, or not. It could have been a rumor he started to flush us out in the open."

"You're right. I'm not going anywhere with anyone unless they show me an FBI badge. No way, I'm going into one of those rooms with any of those so-called security officers."

One of the security guards looked at Patti.

Their gazes met. His eyes widened in surprise. He marched towards her.

Patti grabbed Maria's arm. "Let's go."

The women took off in the opposite direction.

The yacht came close to the pier and then thudded to a stop.

Patti looked at Maria. "We made it. We've got to get out of here."

"I thought you were going to find the FB—"

"Forget it. I just want to get as far away from this place as I can."

Maria's lips trembled and she wiped away tears. "I've got to find Layla."

"We will. We will. Which way to the ramp?"

Maria looked around and pointed. They weaved their way through the dwindling crowd.

Patti bumped into someone and looked up to apologize. She found herself staring directly into the eyes of Raymond Hammond.

34

Raymond's eyes widened in surprise.

Patti froze. She couldn't breathe.

He grabbed her before she could move. "Nice to see you again, Patti. I've been searching everywhere for you. You didn't actually think you could get away from me, did you?" With those words, something pushed against her back. He whispered, "I've got a gun. Don't move."

Patti yelled, "Run, Maria, run."

Maria's head jerked around. Her mouth fell open as she saw Raymond.

"Don't do it, Maria," growled Raymond as he moved the gun up to Patti's head.

Patti stopped struggling as the gun pressed against her temple. *This was it. So close to freedom, only to be caught once again.*

Maria ran several steps, but then slowed and turned back towards them.

"Go, Maria. Just go. Don't worry about me."

A gleam of hatred burned in Maria's eyes as she gazed at Raymond. Her eyes narrowed and her look of hatred turned to terror. She pointed towards them, and screamed, "Gun. He's got a gun."

Heads turned, and then the crowd panicked.

People screamed and pushed to get away from Raymond. The crowd grew in size as the panic increased.

The more Maria screamed, the more frenzied the crowd became.

Raymond muttered an oath.

The gun moved away from her head as he aimed it at Maria.

She had to stop him. Patti hit his arm just as he pulled the trigger.

The gun exploded, terrifying the already panicked crowd even more.

More shots.

More screaming.

People ran and shoved each other as they tried to get away.

Patti looked over to where Maria had been standing. Her heart sank.

Maria lay on the deck moaning, as a puddle of blood formed.

Raymond dragged Patti backwards through the terror-filled crowd towards the exit ramp.

Patti struggled and hit out at Raymond, but to no avail. Her wig fell off as she thrashed about.

"Patti." A voice yelled.

Thank you, God.

Carter stood several feet away from her with his gun leveled at Raymond.

Carter was here—with her.

Raymond squeezed her neck tighter. "Don't be a hero. First, I shoot the woman, and then I shoot you. Just walk away. This is no concern of yours."

Carter didn't lower his gun. Instead, he took another step towards them.

Raymond's arm tightened around her throat.

Carter's gaze met hers for just a moment, and then returned to Raymond. He shook his head. "It's not going to happen that way. You're going to let go of her, and then you get to live. That's the deal."

"I don't like that deal." As Raymond spoke, he twisted Patti's neck and moved further into the crowd.

The crowd quieted and parted. All eyes were focused on Carter and Raymond.

She saw stars and couldn't breathe. Her knees buckled, but Raymond held her up. He slowly backed through the crowd, pulling her with him as he inched his way towards the exit plank.

"You don't think the FBI will let you leave, do you?" Carter asked. "They're waiting for you on the dock."

"They will, if they want her to live." Raymond took several more steps backwards, dragging Patti along with him.

Barely able to breathe, she clawed at his arm.

Carter moved forward.

She heard Raymond cock the gun.

"You take one more step and I shoot her." Raymond's voice was cold as ice.

Her gaze flew to Carter, but she knew he couldn't stop the inevitable.

She steeled herself.

"FBI." A voice behind them called out.

Raymond's head snapped towards the voice. The gun shifted ever so slightly away from her head as he moved.

In the same instant, Carter leaped through the air and tackled the two of them. Carter's arms went around her. His hands found Raymond's.

She felt fingers being pried off her arms and then Carter twisted Patti out of Raymond's iron grip.

More shots.

He rolled her away from Raymond, using his own body as a shield. "You're OK. I won't let him hurt you," Carter whispered in her ear.

She never wanted to leave the warmth and security of his arms.

Carter adjusted his arms, pulling Patti to her feet.

She looked around wildly. "Where is he?'

Carter shook his head. "I don't know. He disappeared into the crowd. The FBI won't let him get away."

She shook her head. Her words were breathless as she tried to gain control of her emotions. "That man is Raymond Hammond...Rahmed Hamed, Joseph's brother. He's the leader. You've got to stop him. He...he...he's dangerous." She took a deep breath. "He killed Jamie."

❧

Carter held her close.

Her head fell against his shoulders. She wanted to stay there forever. Shut out the ugliness of the world, but she couldn't. "What about Maria?"

The FBI was quickly taking control of the crowd that remained on the yacht.

Three different pockets of EMS workers crowded around three different people—Raymond's victims.

Patti moved out of Carter's arms and ran from group to group until she found Maria.

Two EMS workers knelt down beside her. One was attaching an IV, the other pressed against a gunshot wound to staunch the blood.

"I'm right here, Maria."

Maria's eyes flew open and their gazes met. She

managed to gasp out only one word. "Daughter."

Stricken, Patti nodded. "I know. I'll go find her. I promise."

Patti jumped up.

Carter was right there.

Grabbing his arm, she led him away from the noisy crowd. "Raymond kidnapped Maria's daughter. I've got to go find her. "

"Don't worry; he's not going to get off this boat."

"He's probably already on his way. We've got to get there before he does. He'll take her and she'll never see her daughter again. She saved my life." Patti shook her head. "I promised Maria I would find her daughter. I'm keeping that promise."

Carter opened his mouth, but Patti didn't have time to argue with him.

Without another word, she turned and pushed her way past the guards, who had lost control of the crowd when the shooting began.

Carter took hold of her elbow, leading her through the crowd. At the ramp, he held up his badge to the security guards, who nodded and let them pass.

"I have the address. The little girl is supposed to be there. Her name is Layla."

"Let me call Marcus." He pulled his phone out and gave Marcus an update. "Done. The police are on their way.

"I'm going."

Carter touched her cheek. "Are you sure I can't stop you from doing this?"

"No."

"Then, let's go. I'm not letting you out of my sight again."

She went up on her tiptoes and kissed him on the

cheek. "Thank you."

"Come on. I have the keys to the car that Marcus and I were driving."

They ran to the car and jumped in.

Carter programmed the GPS to the address they needed and they took off.

35

She turned towards Carter as they drove down the narrow streets. "How in the world did you get here so fast? I called you in Palm Beach."

His hands clenched the steering wheel. "I wasn't in Palm Beach, I was on a police boat headed to the yacht. As soon as I discovered you weren't in the hotel, I knew you'd found out where Jamie was working. I found the letter with the address. You left it at my house. I grabbed the first plane possible because I…I knew God wanted me to get out here to help you."

"I can't believe you're here." She touched his arm.

"I wasn't going to let anything happen to you." His gaze met hers. His held a promise for the future.

She looked away. Her emotions were in overdrive and she couldn't focus on the future. Her only concern was to find Layla.

❧

Carter flipped his phone shut, his expression grim. "They still can't find the man on the yacht. But there are so many hiding places it could take hours to find him."

"He's not there. I'm telling you, he got away. The man is pure evil. I looked into his eyes." She shuddered. "We've got to get to Layla before her father does. If Raymond gets Layla, Maria will never see her daughter again."

Lillian Duncan

They arrived at a benign-looking house.

Patti pointed to it. "That's the address."

It didn't have a picket fence, but it certainly could pass for the American dream. It was a simple blue house surrounded by a well-manicured lawn. It definitely didn't look like a house where terrorists lived.

Carter pulled into the drive.

"You stay here," he told Patti, but she was already out of the car.

Carter jogged to the front door and rang the doorbell.

Patti watched from the drive as he rang it again and again. No answer.

Please God. Let them be here.

Carter ran back down the steps. "I'm going to check the backyard."

Patti ran to keep up with him. As they rounded the house, the backyard came into view. She breathed a sigh of relief.

Two little girls played on a swing set.

"Layla," Patti yelled.

A beautiful, dark-skinned little girl looked up from the swing set.

The resemblance to Sabrina was eerie. If she'd had any doubt that Joseph Hamed was Sabrina's father, it was gone.

Patti ran to her. "Layla, your mommy sent me to get you. She wants to see you."

The girl smiled. It was the exact same smile as Sabrina. "I want my mommy."

Patti reached out her arms. "I know you do, sweetheart. Come with me and I'll take you to her."

Layla slipped off the swing and walked towards

Patti.

A woman came rushing to them. She had long black hair, olive-colored skin, and wore a simple dress that fell to her ankles. Her black eyes were filled with concern as she looked at these strangers who had invaded her backyard.

"No, Layla, you can't go with her," her voice was calm, but firm.

Layla stopped moving. She looked back and forth between Patti and the other woman, her confusion evident on her face. "She's going to take me to Mommy. I want to see my mommy."

The woman started towards Layla, but stopped as Carter pulled out his gun and flashed his badge.

Still, she didn't give up. "Layla, what did your mommy teach you about going with a stranger?"

The little girl frowned at the woman and then looked back at Patti.

Patti could tell Layla was torn.

She obviously was missing her mother and wanted to go to Patti, but wasn't sure if she should.

Carter walked up behind Patti and slipped something in her hand.

She looked down. It was his badge. She knew just what to say. She showed it to the little girl. "Layla, I'm not a stranger. I'm the police. Didn't your mommy teach you that it was OK to go with the police?"

The girl nodded and took a step towards Patti, but then suddenly yelled, "There's Daddy." She changed direction and ran.

Patti lunged for the little girl, but it was too late.

Raymond bent down and picked up his daughter.

His black eyes gleamed with triumph and fanaticism as he stood back up and looked at Patti and

Carter.

Carter moved in front of Patti with gun drawn.

The other little girl was crying.

Layla's babysitter's head moved back and forth between the men holding guns. She gathered her own daughter into her arms, fearful and protective.

Patti breathed a sigh of relief and focused her attention back on the men.

Carter moved in front of Patti. "Let her go, Hammond. You don't want your daughter to get hurt."

"She's not going to get hurt. We are leaving and you aren't going to stop us." The man was heartless.

Layla was sobbing and burrowing into her father's shoulders.

Carter couldn't shoot him without putting Layla in jeopardy.

The poor little girl must be terrified.

God, please keep her safe.

Raymond began backing up.

He's going to take her. She'll never see her mommy again.

Carter matched Raymond's retreat step for step.

Patti followed, praying. *Do something, God. Don't let this happen.*

The answer to her prayer came charging at Raymond.

A German Shepherd appeared out of nowhere and ran directly across the yard. The dog jumped on his back without warning.

Raymond fell forward.

Patti ran past Carter and grabbed Layla as he turned to fight off the dog.

Raymond shot at the dog. The dog yelped and let go. Blood poured from its shoulder as it dropped to the ground, whining.

Raymond turned back, enraged, and rushed towards Patti and Layla with gun drawn.

She heard the cock of the hammer, and then the shot. A surprised look crossed Raymond's face, and then he crumpled to the ground.

Patti fell to her knees to shield Layla.

Carter raced towards her and then his arms were around her and Layla, holding them, caressing their faces, as if he needed to touch them to make sure they were alive.

"Thank you, God. Thank you, God." He looked at Patti.

Layla sobbed.

"You're OK, sweetheart. You're OK."

Patti closed her eyes and savored the feeling of safety.

He whispered in her ear. "He's dead. He can't hurt anybody anymore."

Sirens squealed and a moment later the yard filled with men and women wearing FBI jackets.

Marcus yelled orders and took control of the situation.

Two officers were tending the dog, who was now wrapped in some kind of bandage. A patch on their arms said K-9.

A woman agent lifted the sobbing Layla, cuddling her. The little girl reached out for her babysitter, who was still holding her own daughter close. Both women came together, hugging the crying children between them, until their sobs subsided.

Patti sank into Carter's waiting arms once more.

She shifted just enough so that she could see Raymond on the ground, dead.

Patti looked back at Carter. "Jamie's dead. He told me he killed her. He told me." As she said the last words, the tears she had been holding back gave way.

Carter held her tight.

"He kil...killed Jamie. He admitted it." Patti sobbed. She'd never see her sister, her twin, again. Never be able to ask for forgiveness.

"I know." Carter kept his arms around Patti as she sobbed.

When the storm subsided, she looked up at Carter. "You know?"

Carter's gaze met hers. "They found Jamie."

"Where? What happened? I need to see her."

"Some tourists found her...her body in the Everglades."

She gasped, then closed her eyes. *Give me strength, God. I trust you. I know you are here with me now.* "They know it is Jamie for sure?"

He shook his head.

"Maybe, it's not her? They could be wrong."

"The general description matches Jamie." Carter grimaced and shook his head. "Patti, you don't need the details. Just remember—"

"I do. I do need the details. Now tell me."

His hand brushed her hair out of her eyes and he moved closer. "They don't have a positive ID yet, they need your DNA to be sure."

She swallowed hard. The Everglades. General description fit, but couldn't make a positive ID.

Her stomach heaved as she understood the implications of his words.

Carter's hand was on her back, comforting and safe.

She looked up at him. "Take me to my sister."

36

Exhausted, Patti laid her head on Carter's shoulder as the limo moved away from Miami International.

Alligators crawled under her eyelids. She jerked to a sitting position.

"Are you OK?" Carter tightened his hold on her.

He hadn't left her side since the yacht.

The FBI had provided a plane for them.

"I'm a mess right now, but I'll survive this. God is with me—with us. Sabrina needs me."

"Yes, she does."

"Where did you say we were going again?"

"Homestead, Florida. It has one of the nearest hospitals to the Everglades. It won't take us long to get there. Just a few minutes. They'll do a cheek swab and then we can go back to the safe house. To Sabrina and Anna. They're waiting for you."

"I want to see Jamie."

He shook his head, his voice gentle. "You don't want to do that, Patti. That's not the way Jamie would want you to remember her."

"Do you think it matters? I see her that way every time I close my eyes."

"But it will get better. Now, it's just your imagination. If you see the real thing, it may never go away."

She had no energy to argue so she nodded. But she

knew she wasn't leaving that hospital without seeing Jamie. What a stupid waste of her time being angry and bitter. *God, I am so sorry. I will never let unforgiveness keep me from a loved one again. I promise.*

"There it is."

She looked up to see an ultramodern facility. For some reason, she'd just assumed it would be a quaint old-fashioned hospital.

They would have the proper equipment to make the...she closed her eyes for a moment, not wanting to think about what she was about to do and why.

The limo pulled up under the portico and stopped.

Patti reached over and opened her own door. *I can do this. I can do this with God's help. And Carter's.*

Carter walked up to the information booth.

After a moment, the woman pointed to an elevator.

Not waiting for Carter, she headed towards it.

He caught up with her and grabbed her hand.

They rode down the elevator in silence.

A woman stood waiting for them as the doors slid open. She gave them a nervous smile. "I'm Cynthia. I'll take you to the lab."

"I want to see my sister."

"Uh...I...was...uh...told that you were here for a DNA swab, not a visual identification." Her face turned splotchy. She pushed her blonde hair behind her ear and glanced at Carter. She bit her lip for a moment and wouldn't look at Patti. "I really wouldn't recommend it."

"It's her sister. It's up to her."

Patti let out a relieved breath.

He trusted her enough to let her make her own decisions.

"Well, I need to get the DNA swab first and then..." Cynthia took a deep breath. "And then I'll take you to the...to her. Is that OK?"

Patti nodded.

Cynthia held open a door and they walked into a small office. "Go ahead and sit down."

Carter grasped her hand and they both sat down, their knees touching.

The woman grabbed a package off the desk and ripped it open. She held up what looked like a giant Q-tip. "I'm going to rub this on the inside of your cheek."

Patti opened her mouth and waited as Cynthia swabbed her cheek. It was over in less than a minute.

The technician put the swab in a glass tube and screwed the lid on it. "Let me just take this to the lab and then...are you sure you want to do this?"

Patti bit her lip. No, she wasn't sure at all. "I am."

"I'll take you as soon as I come back from the lab." She walked out the door.

Patti waited for Carter to tell her not to do it.

Instead, he just squeezed her hand.

The door opened. A nurse stepped in holding a clipboard. "I was looking for Cynthia."

Patti looked up. "She'll be right back."

The nurse threw a glance her way, but then the clipboard clattered to the floor.

Carter dropped her hand and knelt down to get it. "Here let me help you."

He tried to hand it to her, but the woman stared at Patti, not noticing Carter.

"Why are you down here?"

Patti licked her lips and forced herself to say the words. "I'm here to identify my sister."

"Well, you're in the wrong place. This is the

morgue."

"I know that."

"You think your sister's in the morgue?"

"We were told to come down here." Carter told her. "They took a DNA swab and—"

"You're in the wrong place." The nurse ignored Carter and smiled at Patti. "Follow me, please."

They didn't want her to see Jamie, but it was none of their business. Jamie was her sister. "But—"

She crooked her finger at Patti. "No buts. Come with me." Her tone was firm, but she smiled as she said the words.

Carter held out a hand and she reached for him. Their fingers interlocked and they followed the nurse to the elevator, which was open and waiting for them.

"I don't understand. The nurse already took the swab. I want to see my sister. I'm not leaving without seeing her. I have a right to see her. I don't care what anybody says."

"I'm not trying to keep you from seeing your sister." The nurse kept walking. "I'm taking you to her."

The elevator doors slid open. The nurse turned to Patti. "Come on. Let's go." She glanced at Carter, her voice all business. "You can come, too."

Carter squeezed Patti's hand as the nurse hit a button on the wall. The automatic door opened.

Patti took a deep breath, the smell of antiseptic emphasized where she was. Her stomach grew queasy and her knees shook. Maybe, Carter was right. She didn't want to see her sister this way. She didn't want this to be the last memory of her twin. Her hand clenched Carter's. "I can't. Not a good idea."

The nurse turned back and grabbed her hand. "It's

a great idea."

"Look, if she doesn't want to see her sister, then..."

Ignoring Carter, the nurse pulled Patti down the corridor. At the nurse's station, she dropped Patti's hand and walked over to a man in a lab coat, probably another doctor. The nurse whispered to him.

He nodded and looked over at Patti and Carter.

Whatever their conference was about, it gave Patti time to breathe. She looked over at Carter. "I don't know what to do."

"You don't have to do anything you don't want to do, Patti. And you already know what I think, but I'll support you, either way."

Another nurse joined the conference. They were all staring at her as they whispered to each other, nodding and throwing nervous smiles in their direction.

What was wrong with these people? Didn't they know how to deal with grief-stricken family members?

The man said something and then walked over.

The nurses followed behind him with silly grins.

Patti chose to forgive them and not take offense.

They were just nervous. Obviously, they expected her to fall apart when she saw Jamie's...Jamie. And they were probably right.

"I'm Doctor Terry. I'll take you to your sister."

This was her last chance to turn back. Could she live with what she was about to see? *Give me wisdom.* Her mind calmed. She couldn't live without seeing Jamie again, no matter what. Feeling like a zombie, she followed the doctor, Carter close by her side.

The doctor stopped at a cubicle. Monitors beeped.

A patient lay in the bed.

"Is that your sister?"

Patti's gaze followed his finger to the patient in the

bed. Her knees buckled, but Carter was there holding her up and guiding her towards the bed—to her twin. She was bruised and battered, but it was Jamie.

"Jamie.' Patti's body shook with sobs.

Dr. Terry stepped forward. "We weren't able to get an ID on her. She's been in a medically-induced coma but we're in the process of bringing her back. In fact, I was here waiting for her to regain consciousness."

"I was told to come here for a DNA swab, that my sister was dead."

"Obviously a mix up in communications. The police also pulled an unfortunate young woman out of the swamp, who later died." The doctor's face showed compassion. "But as you can see, your sister is quite alive. Thank God the nurse went down to speak with Cynthia about a report—she thought at first you were your sister, and had somehow miraculously recovered. You two bear a striking resemblance to each other."

"We...we're identical twins." She looked at Jamie again. "Is...is...she going to be OK?"

The doctor nodded. "Should be, barring any unforeseen complications. I'm cautiously optimistic."

She squeezed Carter's hand. "It's a miracle."

He smiled back. "It certainly is."

Patti looked up at the doctor. "Can I hold her hand?"

"Sounds like a great idea to me."

Patti gently picked up her twin's hand and leaned close. "Jamie, I'm here. Hurry and wake up. I have so much to tell you."

Someone brought her a chair and she sat down. She held Jamie's hand and prayed.

Finally, Jamie's eyelids fluttered and she squeezed

Patti's hand.

Patti said the words she'd thought she'd never be able to say again. "I love you, sis."

EPILOGUE

Palm Beach, Florida
July 4th

"We need more hamburgers." A voice called.

Carter laughed as he flipped another burger onto a bun. "Are you kidding me? How many burgers can one man eat, Marcus?"

"Don't worry about it, Caldwell. Just keep cooking."

Patti smiled as she wheeled Jamie out on the patio.

Sabrina squealed in the pool.

What a difference a few weeks could make.

Her sister had been home for a few days and insisted on having a barbeque at her house.

The doctor assured them there would be no permanent damage from the beating, but her broken leg kept her in a chair.

Marcus sat at a table with his beautiful wife, Olivia.

Their two boys were in the pool with Sabrina.

"Anna has made a mountain of food. So everyone better eat up."

Jamie turned and grabbed Patti's hand. "Isn't this wonderful, sis?"

Tears threatened, but she managed to choke out her agreement.

ॐॐ

The sun dipped below the horizon as Patti sat on Jamie's patio alone.

The others had left for the beach already, but she'd helped Anna with the cleanup detail.

She let out a contented sigh.

God had been merciful and spared her sister.

Across America, her fellow countrymen celebrated their nation's birthday and their freedom, once again.

Patti had learned the cost of that freedom. And she would never again take it for granted.

When the story of the foiled terrorist plot hit the news amidst the benefit shooting, it had been a media circus, but thanks to Marcus, Jamie and Patti's names were never part of the story.

More than one hundred people had been arrested in conjunction with the ongoing investigation.

Maria was still in the hospital. Patti and Jamie had everyone saying prayers on her behalf every day.

Layla was in a secure location, but Jamie had offered a safe haven for both Maria and Layla once everything settled down.

Raymond was dead, but the FBI couldn't guarantee there might not be others out there looking for revenge.

A hand touched hers. She clasped it and looked up into Carter's sparkling green eyes.

She squeezed his hand and smiled up at him.

"Come on. Let's get to the beach before the fireworks start."

Patti looked up at the ever-darkening sky. Stars were beginning to twinkle along the dusky horizon. She stood up and they walked hand in hand.

He stopped and turned her towards him just before they reached the beach gate. He took her in his arms and she smiled up at him. His lips touched hers, soft and sweet. He was a man to be trusted. He'd proven that to her in ways no man ever had.

She leaned closer and kissed him back.

The earth shook as fireworks filled the night sky.

As they separated, he looked at her with that charming smile. "Now that's what I call a kiss."

"Hopefully, the first of many."

He hugged her close.

She closed her eyes, savoring the moment.